TEA CAN BE DEADLY

SAGE GARDENS COZY MYSTERY

CINDY BELL

ISBN- 13:978-1977551443

ISBN- 10:1977551440

 Created with Vellum

CONTENTS

*F*ull, round, dark clouds weighed down the sky that stretched out across Sage Gardens. A soupy mixture of moisture and heat surrounded the four friends as they made their way along a pristine white sidewalk. A few other people dotted the well-tended paths that sprawled out in various directions throughout the retirement community. Samantha glanced up at the sky for a moment, and smiled. To her, it was the perfect setting for the mysterious and exciting experience they were all about to have.

"Isn't this great?" She turned her attention to the three people that walked with her. Despite her enthusiasm, the others seemed far more subdued.

"I still don't see why I have to come along." Eddy quickened his pace to match hers. "I've told you already, I'm not interested in any of this." His weathered features aligned into a classic Eddy expression of disinterest and mild irritation. When Samantha had first met Eddy, it was as if his years of being a police officer had hardened him to the point that a positive attitude was not a possibility. However, she now knew that he had a softer side, but it took some effort to expose it.

"Eddy, I'm not asking you to believe in it, I'm just suggesting that you be open to a new experience. Besides, what can it hurt?" She nudged him with her elbow and offered him her most cheerful smile. "Won't you do it, for me?" She fluttered her eyelashes and pouted.

He rolled his eyes and shoved his hands in his pockets as he huffed. His shoulders rounded forward as if he was doing his best to disappear.

"Cut it out, Sam, I'm here, aren't I?" His footsteps fell heavier on the sidewalk.

"You know, Eddy, as far-fetched as it may seem, there have been several studies conducted that have proven the validity of some psychic abilities." Walt placed his hand out in front of him and stared at his palm. "There is more to life than just what we can see and touch. Some of the greatest mysteries still persist. What is the meaning of life? Is there life on other planets? How did our planet come to exist? Sure, there are plenty of theories with lots of research, but can anyone really answer any of those questions with absolute certainty?"

"I don't need certainty, just rational thought." Eddy drew his lips into a tight line. "I learned long ago not to wonder about things that I would never find the answers to. It makes you restless."

"That's for sure." Samantha sighed.

Walt peered up at the sky for a moment. "I do believe we're going to get rained on. You know, there was a time when prediction of the weather was considered impossible. I'm just saying, you can't dismiss all of the studies."

"Studies or not, it's a bunch of hooey." Jo stepped up beside Eddy. "I'm with Eddy on this one. If anyone says they know more about me or my future than me, I know they're a con artist."

"All of them?" Samantha looked over at her good friend. If anyone could sniff out a con artist, it was Jo. She'd had a lot of experience with criminals from when she worked as a cat burglar herself. Now that she was reformed and just another retiree that lived within the manicured landscape of Sage Gardens, her past expertise fascinated Samantha.

"Every single one I've ever met." Jo arched an

eyebrow as she tugged her long, black hair back into a ponytail to protect it from the rain. "And I've met quite a few. It's a popular and fairly easy con."

"Although, I do agree with you, Jo, I have to say there was a case I once worked on that left me questioning things." Eddy adjusted the hat on the top of his head and straightened his shoulders some. "To this day I'm not sure how, but a psychic consultant was able to pinpoint the location of a body, and indicate who the suspect was. Once we had that information we were able to gather the evidence that we needed to prove the case and it did lead to a conviction. But other than that one incident, I have not seen an honest psychic, and she certainly didn't read any tea leaves."

"I wrote an article about one once." Samantha eyed the long rectangular building ahead of her. It was the closest building to the entrance of Sage Gardens and served as an all-purpose recreation space for the residents. "All I know is that he was an amazing person. He was so warm, kind, and accepting. I never really decided if I believed in his abilities, but I did believe in the positive impact that he had on other people. His intentions were good, and I suppose, that was enough for me."

"Interesting." Jo tilted her head back and forth.

"Perhaps the comfort of the fantasy is more important than genuine skill in some circumstances."

"Perhaps." Walt paused outside the door. "But I find it is always important to keep an open mind about things. The moment you are certain that you are right, is the moment that you can no longer learn something new." He whipped out a tissue and placed it over the doorknob before he opened it.

"Wise words, Walt." Samantha smiled as he held the door open for her, then Jo, and even Eddy. There were quite a few people inside. Many fliers had been placed around the community over the last week about the opportunity to have a tea leaf reading done. Samantha was excited as she'd never had a reading before. As much as her friends complained, she knew that they were curious, too. But with Eddy's stubborn streak, and Jo's refusal to be the center of attention, she knew that she would have to intervene to ensure that they had a good experience. She waved to a woman in a polka-dot dress who stood a few feet away from the door.

"Hi Samantha." She smiled. "Welcome."

"Hi Betty. Can I pay for four readings please?" Samantha reached into her purse for her wallet.

"Oh, you would like all four in a row?" Betty

laughed. "Let me guess, questions about romance?" She winked at Eddy, who narrowed his eyes.

"No, not all for me. One for each of us."

"Samantha, I told you..." Eddy grumbled, but she cut him off before he could continue.

"Oh hush." Samantha smiled at him. "It won't kill you to try it." She thrust some money towards Betty. "Besides, I've already paid for it. Right Betty?"

"Right." Betty smiled as she took the money. "Come on in, we're set up in the next room." She led them through a set of double doors into a slightly smaller space. There were chairs set up along one wall, some were occupied. In the middle of the room was a small card table covered in a lace tablecloth and candles, along with two small wooden chairs. A woman who appeared to be in her sixties, perched on one chair. She had short silver hair, and a round face with a kind smile. Samantha instantly liked her. She wore just as much lace on her body as was spread across the table. In the chair across from her sat a tall and lanky man. She recognized him from his fire engine red hair which stood out in two puffs above his ears.

"Dale's having his reading done now. Then there are a few people before you, but it shouldn't be too long. You can figure out who wants to go first and let me know." Betty glanced over the group gathered before her. The four were quite well-known in the community, and they tended to stick together.

Samantha could sense Eddy's annoyance, but she decided to ignore it. If she worried about what annoyed him, she would be worried just about all the time. Instead she preferred to be the light in his gloomy point of view, even if that sometimes led to an argument. She knew underneath his tough exterior was one of the kindest and most honest men she'd ever met, and she felt lucky to get to know the real Eddy.

"Thanks, Betty." Samantha smiled. "It's nice of you to organize all of this."

"Oh, it was nothing." She waved her hand.

"So Betty, what made you come up with this idea?" Eddy met her eyes. "It seems like an unusual thing to offer here in Sage Gardens."

"Well, to be honest, I've been dying to have a tea leaf reading. I mean, there are always such great stories about it on television and in the movies."

"What movies?" Jo raised an eyebrow. "I haven't really noticed an abundance of tea leaf readers in Hollywood."

"Oh, you know, there's been a few memorable

occasions over the years." She shrugged and glanced over at the table where Rose spoke quietly with Dale. "I am always on a tight budget though, so in order for me to afford it, having a reading party seemed like the best choice. I figured that there would be some takers around here. Though, I do have to say that I'm rather surprised that you're one of them, Eddy." Betty looked back at him with a smile. "You've always struck me as a bit stuck in your ways."

"Oh?" He folded his arms across his chest. "What would make you say that?"

"Let's see, you follow the exact same routine all the time, spend all of your time with the same three friends, and if anyone gets out of line you're always there to stick your nose into it." She eyed him as a smug smile crept across her lips.

"Oh, she does know you pretty well." Jo laughed, and placed a hand on Eddy's shoulder. She could feel the tension there.

"And it's a good thing he is so quick to intervene, we're lucky to have such a brave man among us." Samantha stepped up beside him. Then she caught sight of Walt, and smiled. "Two brave men, that is."

"Well, Walt is certainly legendary." Betty

winked at him. "I made sure there is plenty of hand sanitizer available."

"No need, I brought my own." He patted the small case at his side. "I never leave home without it. I appreciate the thought, though." He seemed oblivious to Betty's subtle mocking as he walked past her to inspect the rest of the room.

"So, what did make you decide to come here today, Samantha? If it isn't about romance, then what kind of answer are you looking for?" Betty turned her attention back to her, even as Eddy's heavy stare remained upon her.

"I just love trying new things." Samantha shrugged. "It's not as if I expect some life-changing experience, but it's something I haven't tried before, which is always thrilling. I guess in some ways I just miss my career as a crime journalist. At least back then, there was always something new to explore or a risk to take. Now, my riskiest endeavor is whether to have coffee or tea in the morning."

"Tea is always a better choice." Walt smiled as he returned to the group. "If you choose a quality tea the leaves will have been hand-picked, and you have no idea what ends up in the coffee you drink."

"I'd rather not know." Eddy held up his hand. "I mean that, Walt, don't you dare tell me."

"But isn't it better to be informed?" Walt did his best to hold back a smile.

"Walt, I'm warning you." Eddy gave him a stern look. "Some things are better left unsaid, or at least unheard."

"All right, all right." Walt chuckled. "I'll behave."

"Oops, there are some new customers. You four settle in, it shouldn't be long." Betty gestured to the chairs across the room before she headed back to the door.

"Settle in." Eddy nodded. "Just before we get taken for a ride." He walked towards the chairs, with Samantha at his side, and his two other friends following behind. "Samantha, you shouldn't have done that." He frowned.

"I'm just trying to loosen you up a bit, old man." She landed a playful jab to the curve of his stomach.

"Hey, if she wants to waste her money it's fine with me." Jo grinned.

"I just can't wait to have some of the tea. It smells delicious." Walt rubbed his hands together. "Oh, and look there are plenty of cups, that's good. Could you imagine if we had to re-use one?" He shuddered at the thought.

"I'm sure they are very sanitary about it, Walt."

Jo patted his knee. "Just remember, this is all for fun."

"I wonder how much a reading can change a person." Walt gazed at Rose as she remained completely focused on Dale.

"How would it change them?" Eddy cleared his throat. "I imagine it lightens their wallet."

"Not just that way." Walt pursed his lips. "If someone truly believes then every word spoken by a psychic can permanently change their perspective and expectations. Say, if they are told they will get a new and better job, they may begin to spend more money, may even quit the job they have. If they're told romance is just around the corner, they may start dressing nicer, and being more friendly to strangers that might be a potential mate. It's amazing just how much of an impact it can have."

"Good and bad." Eddy shook his head. "It sounds a little dangerous to me."

"Perhaps." Walt nodded.

"I just think it's so interesting, the ritual of it. Did you notice how she's doing everything to the left? She turns the cup to the left, she stirs to the left, I wonder what that is about?" Samantha queried.

"Most superstitions are steeped in ritual." Walt nodded. "It makes it even more intriguing, I agree."

"I think it's just showmanship." Jo shrugged. "A distraction to dazzle the customer into shelling out more cash. If they're busy trying to figure out the purpose of the ritual, then they reveal more than they realize."

"Classic." Eddy grunted. "Such a waste of time if you ask me."

"Well, I guess we'll find out soon enough." Samantha craned her neck in an attempt to see everything she could. Rose offered a warm smile to Dale, then turned the cup over on the saucer. As she did, she gasped, and the cup dropped out of her hand. It clattered onto the table, but did not break. For a long second Rose remained perfectly still with her hand still hovering in the air. Then suddenly she jumped up from the table so fast that she almost knocked it over. The scraping of the chair legs against the floor created quite a screech in the otherwise quiet space. All eyes turned on Rose.

CHAPTER 2

Stunned, Samantha started to open her mouth, but she wasn't sure what to say. The moment seemed frozen in time, drawn to a stop by Rose's horrified expression.

"What's happening?" Walt jumped up, his eyes wide and in search of the cause of the upset.

"Something must have frightened her." Samantha clasped at the base of her neck as she realized that she'd been holding her breath. A furtive glance over at Jo showed that she was just as tense, her hands were in fists at her sides.

"Something's not right here." Eddy straightened his shoulders as his eyes darted in search of any danger. Samantha started to step forward, in Rose's direction, but before she could Rose let out a shriek. It was a disturbing sound, amplified by the high ceilings and distant walls. The sound bounced back at them. It was so unsettling that Samantha's stomach began to churn.

"Is she having some kind of medical event?" Jo covered her mouth with one hand and lowered her voice. "Should we call for an ambulance?"

"I don't think so." Walt frowned as he studied her. "She doesn't show any signs of medical distress that I can see."

"That doesn't mean they're not there, though." Jo lowered her hand again. "She might be having a breakdown."

Still rigid in front of the table, Rose blinked, and drew a trembling breath. She started to back away from the table.

"What is it?" Dale stood up from his chair as well, his long, thin frame tense with determination. "What does it say?" His voice grew stern as he stared at Rose.

"I'm sorry, I can't." Rose covered her mouth with one hand. Her voice was distorted by the force of a sob. Her entire body shook.

"I paid for a reading." Dale put his hands on the table on either side of the saucer and gazed intently at her. "I expect to get a full reading. Whatever you think you see in that mess, I want you to tell me. I deserve to know."

"No, I can't." Rose shook her head and started to turn away.

"What is it? What do you see?" He snarled and slammed one hand down on the table. The force of the blow caused the saucer and cup to jump and clank together. "I'm not leaving here without the truth. Just because you don't like what you see doesn't mean I don't have a right to know what it is."

Eddy started towards them. "That's enough, Dale, time to drop it." His voice cut through the shock that filled Samantha's mind. Something had gone terribly wrong, of that she was certain.

"Rose, are you okay?" Samantha tried to meet the woman's eyes.

"Stay out of this, Eddy!" Dale barked and turned to face Eddy. Dale was a few years younger, and a few inches taller, but that didn't intimidate Eddy. He fixed him with his most authoritative stare and lowered his voice to an even growl.

"The reading is over, Dale. Now drop it!"

Dale turned back towards Rose, but she had already broken into a full sprint towards the door. She didn't speak to or look at anyone she passed.

Samantha caught her eye once, but it was as if Rose looked right through her. Betty, who'd just stepped back into the room, caught her near the door.

"Rose? What is it? What's wrong?" She grabbed the petite woman by the slope of her upper arm to try to stop her from getting through the door.

"Let go of me!" Rose ripped her arm free and charged through the door. She didn't offer any explanation.

"Rose!" Betty hissed her name. "You can't do this to me! You promised me that you could handle this! Everyone here knows me!"

"I have to go!" Rose slammed the door closed behind her. The sound clapped through the room like thunder.

"What happened?" Betty stared around the room for an explanation. Samantha didn't know how to respond. She really had no idea what had happened.

Dale stalked towards Betty with a fierce scowl.

"I want a refund, you hear me? She promised me a reading, then had a little melt-down. Now, I didn't pay to witness that. I paid to hear my reading. I'm not going to get that, so I want my refund."

"Dale?" She stared at him. "Did you do something to upset her?"

"Did I do something?" He laughed, a cruel and dark laugh. "She's the one who screamed in my face. She's the one that took off like she'd lost her mind. All I did was pay for the reading and sit there, like a fool. I should have known better. She's probably a scammer, just like all the rest. See what you brought here, Betty? You should be more careful about the company that you keep."

"Dale, just calm down. I will give you your refund." She began to rifle through the pouch wrapped around her waist. "I have no idea what got into Rose. I'm sorry for that."

"I think it's ridiculous that I came in here just to be humiliated. Is it supposed to be some kind of game?"

"No, it wasn't supposed to be. I'm sorry, again." She held out some money to him. He snatched it from her hand.

"Do me a favor, when you see her again, you tell her that she's terrible. She knew she had me hanging by a thread and then she just took off. Who does that?" He shook his head, then stormed past Betty and out the door. Betty stood there, clearly shaken.

"Betty, are you all right?" Samantha walked over to her. "Is there anything I can do?"

"Explain how all of this went so wrong?" She sighed. "Excuse me, I need to see if I can find Rose. Just give me a few minutes." She headed back out through the door. Samantha turned back towards her friends. The adventurous day she had planned for all of them had certainly taken an awkward turn. She could tell already by the gleam in Eddy's eyes that he was amused by the entire scenario. Of course, he would tell her how he was right about the tea leaf readings being a silly idea.

"I have to say, I never expected to have such a good time." Eddy rocked back on his heels and smiled.

"A good time?" Samantha stared at him.

"Sure, it was quite entertaining." His eyes sparkled as he met hers. "Mostly, the part where Dale nearly lost his mind over the reading. A bit obsessed, don't you think? I'll keep that in mind going forward."

"Well, Rose was in the middle of his reading. Who knows what she said to him just before all of that happened. Maybe she was telling him something very important."

"Or maybe Dale told her he was out of cash and she realized she needed to bail out of the reading because she wasn't going to be able to wring another penny out of him." Eddy raised his eyebrows.

"Ugh, Eddy. Do you always think the worst of people?" She rolled her eyes and walked over to join the group again.

"Not all people, just people that are clearly bad." He followed after her.

"Rose didn't appear to be a bad person." Walt crossed his arms. "From her mannerisms she seemed mild-mannered and warm at first."

"At first." Eddy nodded. "When there was still potential money to be had."

"Eddy, you know usually I'll side with you on something like this, but if she's all about the money, then why would she take off? She would have made plenty of money from other readings throughout the day." Jo shook her head. "It doesn't make sense."

"I guess you're right." Eddy nodded.

"So, what was all of that really about?" Jo placed her hands on her hips as she stared towards the door.

"I'm not sure." Samantha frowned. "Maybe she saw something in the tea leaves that frightened her in the reading?"

"Or maybe she realized that she wasn't fooling Dale? Maybe that's why he was so aggravated?

Maybe he picked up on the con?" Eddy narrowed his eyes. "Whatever it was, she took off pretty fast."

"She did seem very shaken, though. I'm not sure that anyone could fake being that upset. Did you see how pale she became?" Walt walked towards the door. "I do hope she's all right." He peered out through the window into the outer room.

"I'm sure she's fine." Jo cleared her throat. Despite her confident words, she couldn't hide the concern in her voice. "But it does seem very strange. Some people do have mental health problems, I hope that's not what she's dealing with."

Samantha barely heard her friends speak as she remained focused on the cup and saucer on the table. If something had upset Rose, she wanted to find out what it was. She crept up to the table and pulled out her cell phone. The gob of tea leaves on the saucer looked like nothing more than a gob of goo. How could that frighten anyone? She snapped a few pictures of what she saw. As she gazed at each image she noticed that the goo did seem to have a shape to it. The more she looked at it the more certain she was that it could resemble something, but she couldn't place just what. She'd never really thought about how difficult it could be to interpret the leaves. In her mind they just formed a shape or a symbol. But this was far different from that. It was just a pile of wet leaves. As she finished taking pictures, she tuned back into the conversation between her friends.

"All I know is that if someone reacts like that, there's usually a reason." Walt turned back to the others.

"Or she's just a very good actor." Jo shrugged. "It's possible that she wanted to create some kind of scene. You know, a bit of distraction or drama. Either to draw attention, or to deflect it."

"But why would she want to draw attention to her abandoning a reading? What could it be distracting us from?" Walt shook his head. "It doesn't make sense to me. Samantha, what are you doing over there?"

"Just taking some pictures." She snapped two more of the table and the pushed-back chair, then walked back over to her friends. "I thought maybe we could figure out what upset her." She skimmed through the pictures she'd taken to be sure she hadn't missed anything.

"You mean you want to do the reading your-self?" Eddy smiled and met her eyes. "You just can't resist a mystery, can you?"

"Well, the suspense is killing me." She gazed

back at him. "Are you really going to tell me you're not the least bit curious about why she reacted that way?"

"The only thing I'm curious about is why Dale got so upset when she wouldn't finish the reading. You would think he would just shrug it off and ask for his money back. It seems like a bit much for him to be so angry. I thought for a second there we were going to end up in a fistfight."

"That's true. It was quite an overreaction." Walt peered at Samantha's cell phone. "Those are some good pictures. We might just be able to find out something from them."

"What do you think there is to find out?" Jo rolled her eyes. "It's a scam, the whole thing is just a scam. Even the blowup at the end probably has some kind of angle."

"It's not necessary to be so cynical, Jo." Samantha flung an arm around her shoulders. "We all know that you're just upset that you've missed your chance to find out about your future."

"Trust me, the last thing I want to know about is my future." A brief tension passed across her face. "I prefer to live in the moment."

Samantha studied her. She wondered what

might be on her friend's mind. But Eddy's voice drew her attention back to him.

"Well, at this moment I am ready to find something else to do. Are we just going to stand around all day?" Eddy rubbed his hands together restlessly.

Just then, Betty stepped back through the door. Without a word to any of them she hurried over to the table and picked up the saucer and cup. She carried them over to a sink at the edge of the room, then turned back to face them. She took a deep breath and shook her head.

"I'm sorry, everyone, but it appears the readings will be canceled. I never expected any of this to happen. Of course, I will give you a full refund." She walked over to them as she pulled money from her pouch. "I'm sorry for the inconvenience."

"Don't worry about that." Samantha walked over to her and accepted the cash from her. "Did you catch up with Rose? Is she okay?"

"I don't know." She sighed. "She wouldn't speak to me, and then she just took off again. I have no idea what upset her so much."

"I'm a little worried about her, she seemed so shaken." Samantha frowned. "Maybe I should try to speak to her? She's not a resident here, is she?"

"No, she's not. But I wouldn't worry too much

about her. I know it must have been disturbing to see this, but to be honest, she has a bit of a reputation for this kind of behavior." Betty frowned.

"She does?" Samantha glanced back at Jo, who nodded with a slight smile.

"Yes, apparently she can be a bit eccentric and dramatic. She has a history of being unstable. I just never really thought she would actually act so badly during a reading. Please, forgive me for the bad experience."

"It's all right, Betty." Samantha patted her shoulder and smiled. "You're not responsible for any of this, and it's not a big deal."

"Not at all." Eddy settled his hat back on his head. "No harm no foul."

"Great, thanks for that. I'm not sure everyone else will feel the same way. But what can I do?" She laughed nervously, then walked them all to the door.

"Too bad this didn't go as you had planned." Samantha paused at the door and offered her a sympathetic smile.

"Yes, too bad." Betty rested one hand on the door frame. Samantha noticed a slight shake in Betty's hand before she placed it down. Had Rose's outburst really upset her so much?

"Are you sure you're okay, Betty?"

"Sure, I'm fine. I'm just a little embarrassed. I'll be fine once all of this blows over."

"Okay then." Samantha nodded to her. "Try to have a good day." As she followed after her friends through the outer door and out into the brooding afternoon, she discovered that it had rained quite a bit while they were inside. There were puddles to splash in. She smiled at the thought. Eddy laughed as she splashed through the biggest one she could find.

"You always find a way to have fun, don't you, Samantha?"

"What's life without fun?" She shrugged, then resisted splashing him.

"I'll tell you what, why don't we all look into this mystery together? What do you say, Walt?" Eddy called out to him.

"I say, we go to my house and have some tea after all." Walt smiled.

CHAPTER 3

On the way to Walt's villa Samantha stopped by her own villa to grab her computer. As she headed off to meet her friends she skimmed the sidewalks in search of any sign of Rose or Dale. If she saw either, she intended to have a conversation with them about what happened. However, the only people she saw were other residents, and Owen, the on-site nurse. He waved to her before he stepped into a nearby villa. She smiled and waved back. He was a good friend, especially to Eddy.

Samantha reached Walt's villa and paused on the front porch. It was his favorite spot to sit in the morning. His rocking chair had a well-worn seat and the small table beside it had rings on it from where he'd set his tea cup. It was funny to her that he was so particular about some things, and yet those rings didn't bother him. He often cleaned it, but over the years it had left a permanent mark. She sat down in the chair and took a deep breath of the still heavy air. It seemed like only yesterday that she was hunting story after story without much thought to the danger it put her in. The deeper she could get into the truth about a crime, the happier she was. Now she was faced with the monotony of the same activities each day. If it wasn't for her three friends she was sure she would have lost her mind by now. Instead, they kept her on her toes.

"Hey Sam, what are you doing out here? Walt's going to make us all some tea." Jo smiled as she held the door open for her. "Are you coming in?"

"Yes, I just wanted to look at the sky for a moment." She glanced back at the heavy gray clouds.

"It is sure trying hard to rain again." Jo laughed as she gazed out through the door. "I wish it would just hurry up and get it over with."

A few fat raindrops splatted against the porch railing.

"There you go." Samantha grinned. "You summoned the rain."

"Hurry up and get in here before it turns into a

downpour." Jo held the door open for her as Samantha jumped up and rushed inside.

"Is that rain I hear?" Walt glanced at them from the kitchen.

"Yes, it is, it's about to break loose." Samantha glanced over her shoulder at the front window. "You might be stuck with us for a while."

"Well, I couldn't think of company I'd prefer more." He smiled at her, then nodded to Jo. "Sugar?"

"Yes please." Jo stepped into the kitchen to help him with the tea while Samantha settled at the table across from Eddy. He'd already buried his nose in the newspaper that Samantha suspected Walt only kept around for his sake.

"Anything shocking going on today, Eddy?" She crossed her legs and leaned back in her chair.

"All of this nonsense is shocking. I just don't recall things being this crazy when I was young. Do you?" His brow furrowed. "It's wild."

"I'm still young." She winked at him. "But no, things do seem to feel a bit more tense these days. Some say it's because of the media, but I think it's because of all of the stress. Everyone is always in a rush."

"You're absolutely right, Samantha." Jo joined

them and perched on the edge of a chair. "It's like no one has any patience anymore."

"They need to drink more tea." Walt raised an eyebrow as he brought out a tray with four cups on it. "Speaking of tea, I noticed that Rose was using one of my favorite kinds for the readings. I've brewed all of us some so we can enjoy it. I was quite surprised to smell it as very few tea shops sell it."

"It smells like…" Samantha thought about it for a moment. "Licorice."

"It does, doesn't it?" He smiled and set her cup in front of her. "But don't worry, it doesn't taste like it." He tipped his head towards her computer bag. "Why did you bring that along?"

"I took some pictures of the interrupted reading, remember?" She smiled. "I thought perhaps we could do some research on how to interpret the symbols. I always find it easier to work with a computer for things like that."

"Good idea." He nodded.

"If you can do that, maybe you can give us all readings." Jo grinned and held out her cup for her to see. "I want to know when I'm going to find that one great heist."

"I thought you were retired?" Eddy shot her a look.

"It's a joke." She laughed and set her cup back down.

"Don't tease Samantha." Walt wagged his finger at Jo. "Samantha's right. Tea leaf reading has some standard symbols. If she can figure out what the symbol is she might be able to figure out what upset Rose."

"But I thought we decided that was all an act?" Jo quirked a brow. "It was certainly dramatic enough to be."

"Good point." Eddy set his cup down on the table. "It can't hurt to try to figure it out, right?"

"Right." Samantha grinned. "I was hoping that you might all feel that way. Do you want to help me figure it out?"

"Sure. We've got the whole afternoon to dig in." Jo patted the table. "Pop up the computer."

"Let me see those pictures you took." Eddy held out his hand for her phone.

"There are about ten." She gave him the phone.

"Ten?" He grinned.

"I tried not to miss any details." She smiled.

Eddy began to flip through the photographs. Samantha searched the internet for a good resource about tea leaf reading, while Jo did the same on her phone. Walt continued to take delicate sips of his tea.

"Interesting." Eddy held out Samantha's phone to Walt. "Take a look at this."

"Hm." Walt eyed the picture for a long moment. "Yes, I see what you mean. She dropped the tea cup on its side, as if it was what startled her."

"Why is that interesting?" Jo looked up from her own phone.

"Because the tea leaves are on the saucer already." Eddy pointed out the saucer in the picture. "So, what did she see inside of the tea cup that frightened her enough to drop it?"

"Maybe some stuck to the bottom? Don't they read what is in the teacup not what's on the saucer?" Jo narrowed her eyes.

"I think so," Samantha said.

"I guess you didn't get a picture of the inside of the tea cup, Sam?" Jo asked.

"All right, I might have missed one detail." Samantha frowned. "I didn't think the inside would matter."

"Wait, you got one of it on its side. We might be able to see something in that one if we blow it up." Eddy flipped back to a previous photograph. As he fiddled with the phone, Walt and Jo leaned close to watch.

"No luck." Eddy sighed. "No matter what, I can't get a look inside. Maybe if we had some kind of special graphics program."

"No, I don't think so, you can't see what isn't there, and the inside of the cup isn't part of the picture," Jo said.

"Sorry guys." Samantha winced.

"Nothing to be sorry for, you did a good job." Jo smiled. "We can't be sure there was anything inside the cup anyway. Just because she dropped it, that doesn't mean that's what frightened her. It could have been many other things, including, as always, an act to throw Dale off."

"Have you found anything, Samantha?" Eddy set Samantha's phone down and looked across the table at her.

Samantha nodded as she turned her computer to face them.

"I found a website that lists some symbols. However, it says here there can be many different interpretations and that not all tea leaf readers use the same symbols." She groaned with frustration. "That's not very promising."

"I think it's safe to say that Rose probably

followed the most common symbols. She didn't strike me as someone who has been in this line of work for a long time." Jo pursed her lips. "She seemed to lack confidence."

"What makes you say that?" Walt eyed her curiously.

"She didn't really play the part. The goal is to create intrigue and draw more customers in. She also didn't dress the part." Jo tapped her fingertip on the table. "Most psychics I've known will wear bright colors, flashy jewelry, dramatic make-up. They really play up the visual aspect of the role to keep people distracted from the vagueness of their readings. They also tend to be loud. Loud laughter, or loud gasps. She wasn't. At least not until the end there."

"That's true." Eddy drew a slow breath. "So, she was probably an inexperienced tea leaf reader, maybe she taught herself? Where do you learn something like that?"

"Actually, psychic abilities are rather trendy. There are plenty of establishments that offer classes on how to enhance your intuition." Walt shrugged. "She might have taken some of those. Maybe this was just something she does on the side to earn some extra money."

"Well, no matter where she learned it, I think it's safe to assume that these general symbols will give us an idea of what it is that she saw." Samantha tapped the screen.

"If she saw anything." Jo crossed her legs. "I'm still not convinced."

"Before we can get anywhere with this, we have to figure out what the symbol is. I've tried, but I can't make anything out for certain." Samantha picked up her phone from the table and flipped to the best picture of the mound of tea leaves that she'd taken. Then she expanded it to fill the screen. "Any guesses?"

"It looks like chewed-up gum to me." Eddy cringed. "I'd hate to see that on my plate."

"I thought maybe a bird?" Samantha tilted her head to the side. "If you squint your eyes and just focus on the middle."

"Perhaps we can tell something from the finer details." Walt leaned over the phone and began to count the tiny pieces of leaves. "If we have the exact number we can assess the possibilities of what might be formed by that number of pieces."

"Walt, slow down, I think we've got it." Jo placed one hand on the back of his. He stopped counting long enough to look up at her.

"You do?"

"You do?" Samantha repeated as she met her eyes.

"Sure, it looks like a bird like you said. My best guess would be that you're supposed to look at the outline, not so much the whole picture, but the most distinct portions. Once you said bird, it really stood out to me."

"Let's see if any birds are listed here." Samantha scrolled down on the website. "Oh, maybe it's a raven!"

"Yes, it could be." Jo nodded.

"So, let's see." Samantha began to read the description, then paused.

"What is it?" Eddy leaned forward. "Are you going to tell us?"

"I think this might be the reason that Rose took off. According to this, the raven is a very ominous symbol in a reading. It can symbolize death or great misfortune. If a person receives it in a reading, the reader is instructed to proceed with caution and break the news delicately. Maybe Rose didn't know how to tell Dale what she saw."

"Ouch." Jo frowned. "Sounds like Dale was not in for any fame or fortune."

"Really? All of that from a raven?" Walt

narrowed his eyes. "There are so many more intimidating birds to choose from."

"I don't think the choice of bird is what we need to focus on here." Eddy sighed. "If Rose wasn't faking it, if she truly believed that she was giving Dale a genuine reading, then seeing this symbol in the tea leaves might have been very disturbing to her, especially if she was new to giving readings, as we've assumed."

"Disturbing enough to make her run though?" Jo shook her head. "It's not as if the raven was there for her, right? The reading was for Dale."

"Well, the symbols are just a guide." Samantha bit into her bottom lip for a moment. "It's possible that what she saw was far more than a raven. She might have had a vision, or had some sense of why the raven was there."

"Like a nightmare?" Eddy mused. "She saw something horrific enough to make her flee?"

"It's possible." She nodded. "It's hard to say since we don't know anything about Rose, or even how she conducts her readings."

"I still think we can assume she wasn't doing a genuine reading." Jo crossed her arms.

"Let's say you're right, Jo, that doesn't mean

that she knew that." Walt met her eyes across the table.

"Huh?" Jo stared at him, her eyes wide.

"I mean, it's possible that she was delusional. There are some people who are convinced that they are psychics, and though they have been proven to be wrong, that doesn't change the delusion in their heads. They believe they are right, they believe they are psychic. Maybe Rose truly did experience something terrifying, whether it was a valid psychic experience or not." He smiled some. "It's yet another one of those perception versus reality conundrums."

"Indeed, it is." Samantha closed her computer. "Because all that really matters is what she believed she saw. At least we got to the bottom of the mystery, and of course, we found another one. Is Rose a real psychic?"

"No." Jo narrowed her eyes. "I am definitely not convinced."

"Possibly." Eddy shrugged. "Hey, like I said, I've seen things I can't explain."

"I think it's very likely actually, from the intensity of the reaction that I witnessed. I don't think she faked it, that's for sure." Walt finished his cup of tea. "But that's just my perception, of course."

"What about you, Samantha?" Eddy asked. "What do you think?"

"I think I'd like to find out from Rose myself."

"I imagine she'll turn up eventually." Jo stood up from the table. "Until then, I guess there's not much more digging we can do."

"True." Samantha stood up as well. "The rain has stopped. I should get home. I'd like to do a little more research."

"I'm still waiting for my reading." Jo winked at her, then followed her to the door. "Good afternoon, gentlemen." She waved over her shoulder to them.

"Good afternoon, Jo." Walt followed her to the door. "Would you like my umbrella? In case the rain starts again?"

"No thanks. I don't mind a walk in the rain." She met his eyes. "Don't let Eddy get you into too much trouble."

"I'm just reading the paper!" Eddy called out from behind the newspaper he'd already picked up again.

"We'll be fine." Walt chuckled. He watched as the two women walked off in opposite directions, then closed the door.

∽

Samantha headed down the sidewalk that led from Walt's villa to her own. However, instead of continuing along it, she veered off her usual path and took the longer loop. She thought she might have a better chance of spotting Rose or Dale that way. She was still curious about why Dale got so upset over the reading. He clearly was hoping to experience something when he sat down in that chair. Maybe he wanted to hear positive things about his future. She could understand him being frustrated or annoyed, but instead he was furious. Why would a reading, or the lack thereof, bother him so much? Unfortunately, as she walked along, there wasn't another person in sight. Perhaps everyone had tucked away for the afternoon, or maybe news had spread of Rose's outburst. Though the community could be quite gossipy, it also tended to know when it was best not to interfere.

As Samantha recalled, Dale's villa was not too far from her own. She decided to take a detour towards it. She couldn't exactly go up to the door and knock, but if he happened to be outside, she might discover something interesting. As she approached his villa, she noticed that there were boxes stacked on his front porch. She thought that was unusual since it was a rainy day, and though it wasn't raining at the moment, it could start again at any time. She lingered a few feet away from the porch, hoping that Dale would make an appearance. A few minutes later he stepped out through the door. Samantha held her breath. She had to make a decision. She could either walk away before he saw her, or she could wave to get his attention. She knew that he likely wouldn't want to talk to her, but she didn't think it could hurt to try.

"Dale!" She waved to him as she approached the porch.

"Huh?" He looked over his shoulder at her, then narrowed his eyes. She wasn't sure if he even knew who she was as they'd only exchanged a few words. However, as his expression shifted, she sensed that he at least recognized her from earlier that day. "What do you want?"

"I just wanted to see if you were okay. You seemed so upset after the reading and I..."

"And you want to be nosy, right?" he growled. "You're just like everyone else. You think you know me, but you don't. You don't know anything about me!"

"Dale, there's no need to get so upset. I'm not here to be nosy, I just wanted to see how you are."

She took a step back as he thrust a finger in her direction. There was plenty of room between them, but the violence of the gesture left her unsettled.

"I have nothing to say to you, or anyone else, just leave me alone!" He stomped back into his villa and slammed the door. She jumped at the sound. She knew that he might not want to talk to her, but she didn't expect him to be so angry. She stared at the villa for a moment, then turned and walked away. Clearly, whatever he was upset about at the reading, he was still upset about and she wasn't going to find out anything more from him. She headed back down the path towards her villa, with a mixture of guilt and apprehension. Maybe she shouldn't have stirred the pot, but it also made her nervous to think that Dale was so upset. She didn't like the thought of living so close to someone who seemed to have such a bad temper.

As she neared her villa, she caught sight of a black bird perched in a tree. A shiver coasted along her spine as she remembered the raven. She hurried inside, and closed the door behind her. It was a good thing that Eddy wasn't around, or he would have chuckled at the fact that she was spooked by the symbol they thought might have been in the tea leaves. It just seemed a little more than coincidental to see the bird. Although, she downplayed her own belief in psychics, she'd experienced more than one hunch that had led her to the truth. If Rose was a genuine psychic and she did see something horrifying, then it was possible that horror might still come true. Perhaps it was something from the past, but it could also be something from the future. Was Dale in danger?

Samantha settled herself in front of her computer and looked back at the meaning of the raven. After that she looked up Rose. She was sure that if she was a popular psychic she would have some kind of internet presence. However, after several minutes she realized that there was nothing to find. It was odd to her that Rose would offer to do readings without having some kind of business setup. As she recalled there were no business cards on her table. She double-checked the pictures on her phone to confirm that. After coming up empty, she realized that quite a bit of time had passed. She put together a small meal for herself and settled at the table to eat it.

Samantha's thoughts turned back to the image of the raven. She wondered what might have been going through Rose's mind when she saw it. Was she afraid that Dale would be upset with her if she gave him bad news? She could only imagine what it was like for a genuine psychic to reveal information that people didn't want to hear. She'd been in that position a few times as a journalist. Sometimes uncovering the truth led to difficult conversations and the destruction of good people. There were moments when she considered not revealing the information, but only moments, they always passed. To her the most important thing was getting to the truth. She imagined that Rose might feel the same way. She recalled a conversation with the psychic she'd written an article about.

"Miles, what's the hardest part about what you do?"

"The hardest part is the obligation it places on you when you place yourself between the spirit world and the world of the living."

"Obligation?"

"Yes. When I agree to be a spiritual conduit, I am agreeing to give up my free will. I am agreeing to bring through whatever message is given, without bias, and without altering the message for the sake of my comfort or protecting someone's feelings. It can be a very difficult journey."

Those words had stayed with her over the years, as she could see the pain in his eyes as he spoke them. At the time she noted how honest he appeared to be, and though she still stopped just short of believing that he was a genuine psychic, she was fully convinced that he was a genuinely good person. Was that what Rose felt when she saw the raven, that sense of obligation to reveal the truth? If she did, she'd run away from that obligation.

Samantha could only guess that it would have had to be something quite horrifying to drive her away. She recalled the way Jo spoke about the psychics she knew. It seemed quite different from her own experience. So, which one was Rose?

CHAPTER 4

*A*s usual, the next morning Walt woke up fifteen minutes before six. He didn't need an alarm to wake him. His body clock had been set to five forty-five since he started school as a child. He felt as if he missed out on precious time if he woke any later, although that only happened if he took some form of medication or had trouble sleeping the night before. As soon as he was awake, he thought of something that made him smile. It was never one specific thing, but anything in general that would bring a smile to his lips. Lately, it had been thoughts of one of his three friends. He always made sure he started his day with a feeling of excitement, or contentment, or at the very least laughter.

Once he was out of bed, he used those fifteen minutes to wash up, brush his teeth, and make himself his morning cup of tea. As he walked through his living room he detected a faint scent around him. It took him a moment to place it, then he smiled. It was Samantha's perfume. She never wore much, not like other women who possibly bathed in it, but it was just enough to remember her by. In the past, he might have been annoyed by the interference in his routine, but having Samantha, Eddy, and Jo for friends had helped him to loosen up a little. He still enjoyed his rituals, but he also enjoyed them being part of all of it. By six on the nose he was outside on his front porch, ready to enjoy his tea. He settled in his rocking chair. As he took his first sip of tea he noticed that something was off. Actually, he sensed it. He wasn't sure just what it was, but he couldn't relax. Something was pricking at his nerves and the more he tried to ignore it the more on edge he became.

Finally, he set his cup down and stood up from his rocking chair. The creak in the floorboards of the porch was familiar, the distant chirping of local birds was exactly as it always was, but there was another sound. It was a subtle tapping. It wasn't part of his morning routine. After a second of observation he was able to pinpoint the direction that it was coming from. A villa, two blocks over. The screen door wasn't latched. It rocked back and forth with every light breeze that passed. Once he pinpointed the sound, it seemed even louder, almost loud enough to be a banging. The more he heard it, the more it dug deep into his brain. Every nerve in his body jumped in response to the sound. It just wasn't right. It wasn't part of his morning routine, and it threatened to put his morning out of whack and ruin it.

Walt knew that the villa was empty, it was one of the few for sale in the popular community. The previous owner had decided a move to Florida would be better for himself and his wife, but they had priced the villa quite high. The word around the community was that interested buyers were biding their time, hoping that the price would come down if the villa didn't sell. He kept an extra eye on it due to that, as he knew that any empty structure could become a refuge for a squatter. However, he hadn't noticed any recent activity around the house. So why was the door unlatched? Why was it banging that way? He was surprised that it hadn't woken him. He covered his ears for a moment and took a breath. Yes, it was a problem, but just like most problems it could be solved with a little perseverance. After a few more deep breaths, he lowered his hands and stood up from his chair.

"Maybe a gust of wind loosened it," he said to himself as he left his tea on the small table beside his rocking chair and crossed the distance between his villa and the empty one. "Maybe maintenance left it unlatched." He frowned. It was a simple mistake to make, but it could lead to damage to the door or the door frame. As he made his way up on to the porch he intended to just secure the door. But when he pushed on the wooden surface he caught a strange scent in the air. It tickled beneath his nose, and spiked his nerves instantly.

Candles? His heart skipped a beat. If that was the case he had to go inside and check. It was never safe for a candle to be left unattended and a fire could spread quickly through their community. He pulled the door open and found that the inner door was slightly ajar as well. He nudged it with the toe of his shoe. The door swung open and a stronger scent filled his nostrils. The living room area was empty but for a small table, two chairs, and an assortment of candles that formed a circle around the furniture. The scene reminded him of something one might see in a horror movie. He took a deep breath and thought about calling for help. But what was there to report? A table and chairs? Some unattended candles?

Walt stepped further into the villa. He noticed that there was a cup and saucer on the table. His heart began to pound. Was it Rose that broke into the unoccupied villa? He glanced up, and past the table, towards the hallway that led to the bedroom. When he caught sight of white lace, and silver hair, his stomach twisted. Strewn across the hallway floor was Rose. He recognized her right away, despite the fact that her face was covered with loose dry tea leaves. He gasped and stumbled back. He grabbed on to the wall to steady himself as his legs grew weak and threatened to collapse. The entire world grew wobbly and bent at strange angles. Despite the chaos in his mind, it was clear to him that she was no longer alive.

As Walt fumbled for his cell phone to call for help, tears stung his eyes. He realized after a few seconds that he didn't have his phone with him. As a rule, he never brought it out on to the porch with him for his morning tea. It was a distraction, and he preferred to be as disconnected from technology as he could be in those first few minutes of his morning. Now, he understood why his friends teased him about not always having it handy. He rushed back to the door and threw it open, without regard to a tissue to protect his hand from the germs on the knob.

"Help!" His voice sounded strange and high-pitched to his own ears. "Help!" He yelled again, and this time it sounded a little stronger. He was so dizzy with panic that he couldn't see if there was anyone nearby on the sidewalks. He could only hope that someone would hear his shouts.

～

*W*hen Samantha called Eddy early that morning, he didn't hesitate to answer the phone. He was certain that if she was calling before seven, there was a good reason.

"Samantha? What is it? Is everything okay?"

"Yes, it is. I'm sorry to call so early. I just have so many theories in my head and I need someone to try them out on."

"Theories? Theories about what?"

"About the reading, and about Dale."

"Are you still hung up on that?"

"I just can't shake it. I feel like it's more impor-tant than we think. Yesterday, I saw Dale, he had boxes stacked up on his porch and he was very angry."

"Wait a minute, you saw Dale? When? You saw boxes on his porch?" He paused, and she could tell that he was doing his best to keep his voice calm. "Did you go to his place yesterday?"

"I was curious. I wanted to see if he was still upset, and yes, he was."

"Samantha, you shouldn't have done that. I would have gone with you."

"Right, and the two of you would have probably ended up in a fight. Anyway, are you up for hearing some of my theories?"

"Yes, I'm always willing to listen. But you need to recognize that we may never figure out what all of this was about, and perhaps it was never about anything at all."

"I hear you, Eddy, I do hear you. Will you meet me at the community center?"

"I'll walk with you there. I'll be at your villa in a few minutes."

"Thanks, Eddy."

He hung up the phone, straightened his tie, and grabbed his hat. As he headed out to meet her he wondered what ideas she might have come up with. Whenever he was stuck on something, he would turn to Samantha first for some insight. Whether it was her intuition or just her ability to dig deep into a question, she always seemed able to get to the answer. However, she could also become so preoccupied with trying to find out the truth that she would let everything else fall to the wayside. It was best to help her solve her questions about the readings before curiosity turned into obsession.

"Morning Eddy." Samantha smiled at him as she stepped out of her villa. Her long copper-red hair was braided as usual with just a few strands of gray loosened from the tie's grasp.

"Good morning, Samantha." He waited for her to join him at the edge of the sidewalk, then they began to walk together towards the community center. "Why did you want to go to the community center?"

"I thought I'd check and see if anyone there knows who had a reading. I figured we could get an idea of what Rose's behavior was like before Dale's reading." She shrugged. "It might give us some insight into why she took off the way she did."

"True." He narrowed his eyes as he looked up at the light blue morning sky. "At least it's a nicer day today."

"Much." Samantha started to say more, but a

scream silenced her. It wasn't so much the cry for help that startled her, as it was the voice that she recognized. "That's Walt!"

"Yes, it is!" Eddy ran straight towards the voice. He ignored the ache of his knees and his hips as he broke into a full-force pursuit sprint. In his days as a police officer he'd been known to run down a suspect no matter how fast they were. As he reached the villa, he realized it wasn't Walt's, but there he was in the doorway.

"Eddy, call the police!" Walt stared into his friend's eyes, his voice breathless and high-pitched. "Rose is dead!"

Samantha caught up with Eddy just as he pulled out his phone to place the call. She looked from Walt, to Eddy, and then back to Walt.

"What's going on, Walt? Are you hurt?" Samantha asked.

"No, I'm not. But I'm afraid Rose has been. I found her body just now." His chin trembled. Samantha climbed up the steps to join him on the porch and wrapped her arms around him in a tight hug.

"I'm so sorry, Walt. Are you sure?"

"I'm sure." He lowered his eyes. "She must have been dead for some time. Samantha, it's just awful."

"Yes, I'm sure it is." She squeezed his hand. "You stay out here with Eddy. The police will be here soon. I'll just take a look to make sure that there's no one else inside."

"Samantha, be careful. I have no idea what happened, but my observations tell me that this was no accident."

Walt's words shook her to the core. It was one thing to discover that Rose had died, it was quite another to hear that she'd been killed.

CHAPTER 5

Samantha stepped inside the villa with a tremble in her hands.

"Samantha, get back here!" Eddy huffed as he hung up the phone. "The police will be here any second."

"I'm just going to take a look, I'm not going to touch anything, I promise." She continued into the villa. When she saw the furniture with the ring of candles around it, she realized that things might be stranger than she expected. She snapped some pictures of it, and the rest of the space. Then she saw her, Rose, in the hallway. She took some pictures of the scene around her. When she lowered her phone, and took a good look at the woman she found it quite difficult to hold back tears. No, she didn't know her, but she had just seen her the day before, alive, full of energy, enough to create a dramatic scene. She backed out of the villa just in time to hear Jo's voice.

"Hey, what's all of the commotion?"

"It's not good, Jo." Samantha walked out of the villa as several police cars pulled across the sidewalks and parked directly in front of the villa. In the back of her mind, Samantha felt sympathy for the grounds crew that would have to repair the damage to the grass. However, the thought was wiped from her mind as she pulled Jo aside.

"What's going on here?" Jo's eyes flitted across the police cars to the uniformed men that stepped out. She was still nervous around badges, and hadn't expected to be thrust into the middle of a crime scene.

"Rose is dead. Walt found her body inside. Eddy called the police." She held out her phone. "I took pictures."

"What? Why?" Jo blinked a few times. "Wait a minute, did you say Rose is dead?" She tried to make sense of everything Samantha had said.

"Yes. We'd better get out of the way."

An officer walked towards them with a grim expression.

"Step aside, ladies, we need to tape off the area."

"Yes, of course." Samantha grabbed Jo firmly by the wrist and pulled her off to the side, where Eddy already stood waiting for them.

"I knew I should have slept in." Jo cringed as another police car with its siren blaring drove past.

Eddy looked at both of them as they joined him at the edge of the property.

"This is going to get intense very quickly. I'm not sure why they sent so many cars, but it was a solid and quick response. At least someone is on the ball." He eyed the officers gathered outside for a moment. "Though it seems to me that they have far too many officers here for a simple death investigation."

"Walt doesn't think it's just a death investigation. He said he suspected it was murder." Samantha clasped her hands together as her heart fluttered. Even saying that word made her uneasy. It was always intriguing to her to have a crime to solve, but not when it came at the cost of someone's life.

"Walt certainly has an eye for detail. I imagine he knows what he is talking about," Jo said.

"Sir, you need to stand over there." An officer directed Walt to the edge of the property as well. Walt seemed anxious as he glanced back over his shoulder at the villa, then reluctantly walked towards them.

"Are you okay, Walt?" Jo gazed into his eyes.

"No, I don't think I am. I tried to point out the important parts of the scene in there, and they acted as if I was in the way. How rude is that?"

"Walt, they have a job to do." Eddy fixed him with a steady stare. "You have to let them do it."

"But I…" Walt started to protest, but an officer stepped up behind him and interrupted him before he could.

"Excuse me, sir, you were the one to find the body?" The officer stepped forward with a notepad in her hand.

"Yes." He met her eyes. "Unfortunately."

"May I speak with you for a moment? Alone? I just have a few questions for you." She shifted nervously from one foot to the other. He noticed that she was quite young, perhaps a recent graduate from the academy.

"Yes, of course." He nodded to his friends, then followed her up on to the porch. He was already having a bad day, he didn't see any reason to make hers more difficult.

"Must be a rookie." Eddy shook his head and shoved his hands deep into his pockets. "It's going to take a while. The young ones are always quite determined to do an excellent job so they are very thorough."

"Good." Samantha frowned. "I hope she goes over every tiny detail, because nothing about this makes any sense to me. Why would someone kill Rose?"

"It's probably best not to jump to any conclusions." Jo folded her arms as she leaned back against a nearby pole. "Isn't it possible that this could have been an accident?"

"Why would anybody accidentally spill tea leaves all over themselves?" Samantha asked. "I saw it with my own eyes, Jo. It didn't look like an accident."

"Maybe not at first glance. But isn't it possible that she had a heart attack while she was carrying a bag of tea. Maybe in the shock of it she spilled the tea?" Jo glanced between Eddy and Samantha. "Sometimes there is a simple explanation for things no matter how strange it seems."

"Sometimes. But look at this." Samantha scrolled to a picture. "It looks to me like she had everything set up for a reading. Do you think she was meeting someone there?"

"Maybe, it looks like she'd already done the

reading, or at least prepared it." Eddy pointed to the cup on its side. "Maybe whoever she set all of that up for was the killer."

"If there is a killer at all." Jo pursed her lips. "It could be a ruse gone wrong."

"A what?" Samantha met her eyes.

"See the candles? The ring? It's as if she was trying to put on a show. Maybe she intended to do something flashy, or dangerous to garner a little more cash or respect from her client, but failed. Maybe something went wrong, and it killed her."

"I'm not sure I understand." Eddy narrowed his eyes as he studied the picture. "You think this was all staged?"

"It's possible. I've heard stories of scam artists lighting themselves on fire, hiding fake blood packets to make it look like they've been cut. Yes, and once, there was a story about a woman who used a drug to make herself appear dead, and several hours later, miraculously returned to life." Jo nodded.

"Wow." Samantha's face paled. "I never even considered that. It's possible she took something to create an illusion and died as a result of it?"

"Possible, but farfetched." Eddy shook his head. "She didn't seem experienced enough to do anything like that. And what was she doing here in an empty villa? She risked getting caught. That doesn't make sense to me."

"It doesn't always have to make sense." Jo spread out her hands. "Sometimes people do stupid things and take stupid risks."

"Maybe Walt will know more." Eddy tilted his head towards the porch as Walt stepped back outside. His expression was grim as he wiped a tissue along his palms and descended the steps.

"Walt, how are you doing?" Jo placed her hand on his shoulder and looked into his eyes. The wildness in them left her a little shaken. She knew that if things were out of control for Walt it was hard for him to cope. "Are you okay?"

"No, not at all." He frowned as he looked at the others. "I overheard a few of the officers talking. It was definitely a murder. It looks as if the murderer stuffed tea leaves down her throat and made her choke on them. Who could do a thing like that?"

"Someone trying to make a point, or send a message." Eddy clenched his jaw.

"Yes, exactly that." Samantha balled her hands into fists. "Whatever Rose did, whoever she was, there's no way that she deserved to die like this."

"The question is then, who did it?" Jo glanced

around at the crowd that had begun to gather not far from the villa. It was filled with her neighbors, people she saw every day. Jo wasn't the most social person, so she didn't know all of their names, but their faces were familiar. Could any of them be the killer? It was hard not to consider the possibility.

"Who had access to the villa?" Samantha opened a notepad application on her phone. "That's somewhere we can start."

"That's a good idea." Walt nodded. "It's possible that she broke in."

"We should get you out of here." Jo steered him away from the villa. "I can't imagine how upsetting this must be for you."

"Yes, let's get him home." Samantha fell into step on the other side of him. Eddy trailed behind the three, his brows knitted in deep thought.

～

The four friends crossed the short distance to Walt's villa. As they reached it, Walt paused at the base of the stairs, then looked back at the collection of police cars.

"How strange." He took a breath so deep that his chest puffed out.

"What's strange?" Jo paused beside him and followed his line of sight.

"I've never seen the walls of these villas painted with red and blue. It just made me realize how very different things could be."

"It's all right, Walt, let's just get you inside." Jo rubbed a small circle on his back. "Don't get lost in the details."

"But that's all there is, details." He chuckled a little, as they walked inside.

"Enough." Eddy tapped his hand on the railing. "We have a crime to solve."

"Yes, you're right." Walt ascended the stairs, then paused beside his rocking chair and stared down at his cup of tea.

"It's cold," he muttered, as if puzzled by the thought.

"How about if I make you some fresh tea?" Jo patted the slope of his back. "Hmm?"

"Yes, that would be nice, thank you." He continued to stare at the cup for a moment, then as if he made a decision, picked it up, and carried it inside the villa. The others followed behind him. While Jo prepared fresh tea for everyone, Walt, Samantha, and Eddy gathered around his table. The moment so resembled the afternoon before that

Samantha had to remind herself that everything was actually different. They weren't there to discuss a strange reading, they were there to discuss the death of a woman they'd not even had the chance to meet.

"It's so strange that she's gone." Samantha stared down at her phone. "We were never even introduced."

"It is strange." Eddy narrowed his eyes. "And concerning. Whoever did this obviously had a personal score to settle with her. Otherwise why would anyone have gone to all of the trouble to kill her like that."

"It could have been someone that she scammed." Jo poured tea into four cups, then carried them to the table. She set one cup in front of Walt and met his eyes. "I hope you can enjoy this."

"Of course, thank you, Jo." He spared her a small smile, then gazed down at the tea.

"Maybe someone that she bilked for a lot of cash tracked her down here?" Samantha looked around the table at the others. "Feeling tricked could be a very strong motivation for murder."

"Yes, it could." Walt took a sip of his tea, and smiled at Jo again. "Excellent, thank you."

"My pleasure." She smiled at him in return, then looked over at Samantha. "Or it could be that she was killed by someone who felt betrayed by a prediction that didn't come true."

"It may not have anything to do with the readings at all. Maybe someone just wanted it to look that way." Eddy quirked a brow. "It was quite an elaborate scene for a frame job, though."

"It could also be someone who was angry about the reading itself." Samantha stirred her tea. "We all saw how angry Dale got when she wouldn't finish his reading, and when I spoke with him yesterday he was still furious. Do you think it's possible he came back for another one? Maybe she refused again, and he got angry again?"

"Maybe." Eddy frowned. "I hate to think that Dale could go that far, but I don't really know the man that well. Do any of you?"

"Not me, that's for sure." Jo shook her head. "He's always made me feel a little uneasy so I keep my distance."

"I've talked to him a few times." Samantha closed her eyes for a moment as she recalled the last time she spoke to him. "He's a rather gruff and distant person. Any time I've been friendly to him he's been dismissive and finds a reason to walk away."

"I'm not sure that he and I have ever even

crossed paths." Walt looked thoughtful for a moment. "No, I don't think that we have."

"It sounds like we need to find out more about him. I can look into his past." Eddy made a note on the notepad he always carried. "If he has a criminal past, I'll find out."

"I should really check on Betty." Walt took the final sip of his tea. "I'm sure she will be quite upset. She might have more to say about Rose as well. Maybe none of us know Dale well, but we didn't know Rose at all."

"Are you sure you want to do that?" Jo studied him. "She might not have even heard about Rose's death yet."

"I can handle it." He nodded. "She should have someone friendly nearby when she hears the news."

"Do you want me to come with you?"

"No, that's okay, I'll be fine." Walt knew that Jo wasn't the most sociable of people and she would really prefer not to join him. Besides, he felt Betty would probably be more relaxed if she had the support of someone, but didn't have to face everyone.

"Jo, I say you and I head to the coffee shop on Main. The Sage Gardens Café is closed today, so if there's any gossip about Rose or her death to be found, that's where we will find it. Besides, I'm still curious about others who might have had readings before Dale left yesterday. Maybe they can give us more insight about her routine and whether she was clearly trying to scam them," Samantha said.

"Good idea." Jo began to collect the tea cups.

"It's all right, Jo, leave them. I'll take care of it." Walt smiled at her. "You've done enough."

"I wish I could have stopped you from walking through that door this morning. I know how difficult it must have been for you to see that."

"I'm all right." He held her gaze. "I'm stronger than you think, thanks to my wonderful friends."

"Anything you need, Walt, we're here."

"I know that." He took her hand in his for just a moment, then released it. "Hopefully soon, all of this will be behind us."

"Samantha, do you want to help me search for some information before you go to the coffee shop?" Eddy asked. "Let the news travel around first."

"Sure." Samantha nodded.

"My place, I'll need a coffee and some of the numbers for my police contacts."

"Is that okay with you, Jo?" Samantha asked.

"Perfect, I ran out of my villa this morning and I

didn't have time to get ready properly. Come and get me when you're ready."

"Okay, I'll just pick up my computer, Eddy, and I'll meet you at your place," Samantha said.

As his friends left together, Walt considered just how lucky he was. No, it wasn't pleasant to find Rose that way, but he was glad that he was the one to find her. He knew that he and his friends would do whatever it took to find out the truth.

CHAPTER 6

*E*ddy headed back to his villa, though it was hard to get to as most of the community now populated the sidewalks surrounding Walt's villa. The flashing police lights still bounced off the smooth surfaces of the villas, and official police vans dotted the main parking lot. He could hear the conversations as he passed by them.

"I heard it was Walt."

"No, it wasn't Walt. Walt found the body."

"What? Walt killed someone?"

"No, I heard she died of a heart attack."

"Who died?"

Eddy sighed and lowered his head as he continued to walk. The last thing he wanted was to be bombarded with millions of questions if someone recognized who he was. Finally, he made it to his villa. He knew the rumor mill would only get worse as time passed. The thought of Walt being suspected as a killer made him feel terrible. He knew it would upset Walt if he heard that rumor, and in time, he would. The sooner that they could figure out what happened to Rose the better it would be for everyone.

After turning on the coffee maker to brew some actual caffeine there was a knock on the door. Eddy opened it to find Samantha on the other side.

"Where do you want to start?" Samantha asked as she put her computer on the table and sat at the desk.

Eddy grabbed his cell phone then settled into his favorite well-worn easy chair. As the springs groaned he kicked his feet up and prepared himself for a deep search.

"You see what you can find out about Dale," Eddy said. "I've got some calls to make."

It took Samantha a little longer than usual to track down information about Dale as he wasn't originally from the area. She found out that Dale had lived at Sage Gardens for just over two years. In that time he hadn't had any legal issues that she could find, nor had he any complaints lodged by neighbors. He had moved around several times before he settled in Sage Gardens.

Once she made her way through about ten former addresses she came to one that Dale lived at for over five years. With this address she was able to discover that Dale had some serious financial difficulties for some time. There were bill collectors, as well as some civil court matters regarding failure to pay. She also found that his home at that address had gone into foreclosure, and the bank took ownership. Samantha explained what she had found out to Eddy.

"Poor sap. In this economy, it's hard to stay afloat." Eddy shook his head as Samantha continued the search. When checking his employment at the time, Samantha noticed that Dale had been fired from the warehouse where he had worked for over ten years. Eddy placed a call to the main office of the warehouse. After several rings, he was directed to a voicemail. He decided against leaving a message. It was not likely that he'd find out why Dale was fired, even if someone called him back, as that was information most companies would refuse to give out.

"At first, I assumed that the loss of the house was due to the loss of his job, but maybe there is another reason. Maybe something criminal?" Samantha shrugged.

"Maybe." Eddy nodded. He looked over at Samantha. "Do you want to leave this with me, Sam?"

"Yes, thanks." Samantha stood up. "I would like to go to the coffee shop, now. It should be bustling with gossip." She walked to the door.

"Thanks for your help." Eddy closed the door behind her.

After a few phone calls Eddy spoke to someone that could help. It paid to still have contacts in the police department. He smirked when he found out that Dale had a criminal record. He had no idea what the record was over. After some persuasion, his contact sent through the case file.

He printed the file and started reading through it. He was shocked to find that Dale had been arrested on suspicion of murder.

"Well, well, well," Eddy mumbled to himself as he continued to page through the arrest record. "Someone does have some secrets."

Eddy read over the description of the charges and grew even more uneasy. Dale had been accused of murdering his wife, Anna, who he had been married to for five years. Her body was found in the home they shared. Dale was fired from his job when he was arrested for her murder and had no ability to pay the mortgage while behind bars. Within a few months, the house was foreclosed on and taken.

After a long wait for the trial to begin, Dale was acquitted of all charges. Eddy was stunned that he'd sat in jail for so long waiting for his trial, and that it was so swiftly dismissed once it was started. With so many holes in the case, he decided to take a chance and see if he could get in contact with the detective who investigated the crime.

At the time of the murder Dale was living in Dradford, a working class town about an hour away, which bordered on a wealthy neighborhood called Bright Bay Heights. Eddy found the detective's name on the case file, and placed a call to the Dradford Police Department. After several rings, a gruff but female voice answered the phone.

"Dradford PD, how may I direct your call?"

"Excuse me, ma'am, could you please connect me with a Detective Weiss?"

"Detective Weiss?"

"Yes ma'am, is he available?"

"I think you have the wrong police department. We don't have any Detective Weiss here."

"I'm sorry to bother you, ma'am, but he's listed

on a case file as the investigating detective. Are you sure he has never been a detective there?"

"Oh, well, I didn't look in the inactive records. Let me check." She paused a moment, then spoke again. "Sure, Detective James Weiss was a detective here, but he's been retired for three years."

"Is there any way that I can get in contact with him?" He frowned as he skimmed the case file again. Only the investigating detective would know every detail of the case, and that was the information that he needed.

"I'm afraid we don't give out contact information for our detectives, for their safety."

"I understand. Would it be possible to get a message to him? I'm looking into a case he worked, and if he's interested in discussing it with me I'd love to hear from him."

"Sure, I guess I could do that."

"Great, thanks so much." He relayed the message to her along with the case file number, his phone number, and his years of experience as a police officer. He had no way of knowing whether she would really get the message to Detective Weiss, but he hoped she would. But would Detective Weiss be interested in helping him out? When some police officers retired they wanted nothing to do with the job. That was not the case when Eddy retired. In fact, there were many times when he felt such a desire to return to the force that he considered fighting against the rules that forced him to retire. Hopefully, Detective Weiss felt the same way.

~

W alt took the back way towards Betty's villa. It was a hobby of his to keep track of who lived where in the community. It made him more at ease to have an idea of where everyone was at any given time, though he was not one to stick his nose in other people's business, normally. Still, he guessed that if Betty had heard about Rose's death then she would be quite upset, and if she hadn't, then she wouldn't want to hear it as a rumor from someone who had no idea what really happened. He assumed that they were probably friends, though Betty hadn't said the kindest things about Rose after Dale's reading went sour. He reached the villa without running into anyone else, which was a relief. He did not like surprises.

When Walt stepped up on to the porch he noticed how similar it was to his own. One of the things that attracted him to Sage Gardens the most was its uniformity. He liked that every villa looked just about the same, and even the landscaping was repetitive and carefully coordinated. Things being in order, especially in an even number, always made him feel more at ease. He knocked four times on the door, then stepped back to wait for her to open it. As he waited, he counted the seconds that passed. When he reached sixty, he realized that she might not be home. He counted up to sixty again, then decided to knock once more, just in case she hadn't heard him the first time. He knocked four times again. This time he heard a noise from inside the villa. It startled him amid the silence on the porch. Was it a chair scraping? Not exactly. It sounded like something sliding across the floor, though. A few seconds later, Betty opened the door. The moment he saw her, he knew that she had already been informed of her friend's death. Her eyes were swollen and puffy, and her cheeks were red.

"Betty, I'm so sorry for your loss." He frowned.

She stared at him for a moment as if she might not recognize him, then smiled.

"Walt. What are you doing here?"

"I came to check on you." He folded his hands in front of him. "I'm sorry, I don't mean to bother you, I just wanted to be sure that you were okay. I'm sure it was quite a shock, it was quite a shock to me."

"Then you did find her?" She gestured for him to step inside. "I heard that was the case, but I wasn't sure if it was just a rumor."

"Yes, I'm sorry to say I did find her." He followed her through the door. "I can only imagine how difficult this must be for you."

"It is, so very difficult." She grabbed a box of tissues from a side table and pulled a tissue out. "I keep trying to figure out how it could have happened, but then I get dizzy, because none of it makes sense."

"I understand." He pulled out a tissue himself, placed it over his palm, and then patted the curve of her shoulder, with his skin protected. "I'm sure that the police will do their best to figure out what happened. For now, why don't you let me make you a cup of tea?"

"Oh, that would be wonderful." She sank down into a chair at the dining room table. "A few of my friends have called to see if I need company, but I can't bring myself to ask them to come. I'm just not sure that I could entertain them."

"Well, you don't need to entertain me. Here we are." He pulled out a tin of tea. For a second he froze. He recognized the brand and type of tea right away. It was the same fruit tea that Rose used at the tea leaf reading, one of Walt's favorite teas. "This is such a delicious tea. Do you buy it often?" He glanced over at her.

"Oh, the guy at the tea shop recommended it." She shrugged. "He suggested it. I actually haven't tasted it myself, yet."

"Please, allow me to introduce it to you. It will help, I can assure you." He began to brew the tea. It made sense now that Rose would use the same tea. After all, Gerardo at the local tea shop was quite the expert, and he had commended Walt when he chose the tea the last time he purchased it. He wouldn't hesitate to recommend it to anyone. He finished preparing the tea then brought it to the table and set it down in front of her.

"Aren't you having some?" She met his eyes.

"I've just had a cup not long ago, I have to pace myself." He smiled as he sat down across from her. "Do you mind if I sit with you for a little while?"

"I'd like that very much." She sighed as she grasped the cup. Walt noticed that it was a deep blue shade, far different from the white cups used at the tea leaf reading. He assumed they must have belonged to Rose.

"Forgive me if I'm being intrusive, but had you known Rose long?" He watched as she stirred some sugar into her tea.

"Not too long. In fact, I didn't really know her well at all. I asked Gerardo at the tea shop if he knew anyone that did tea leaf readings. I figured if anyone would know, he would. I'd been wanting to have one done. He suggested Rose to me. We met a few times, and really hit it off. However, her readings were a bit pricey. She offered to do a party for me, so that all of the readings would be at a reduced rate and because I would be hosting it, mine was free. It seemed like a win-win at the time." She closed her eyes for a moment. "Now, all I can think is that maybe if I hadn't ever contacted her, she would still be alive."

"Oh Betty, you can't blame yourself." He reached for her hand, then hesitated. There were some people that he could touch fairly easily, like Jo, Samantha, and Eddy, but most others he had a hard time with.

"It's okay, Walt." She offered him a small smile. "I understand your compulsions, you don't have to touch me."

"I do wish I could offer you some comfort."

"You being here is comfort enough. Thank you."

She took a sip of her tea. "Oh my, this is delicious, just as you said. Fantastic, really."

"It's very smooth and strong at the same time. I find it calms me to the core."

"I hope it does the same for me." She swirled the tea.

"I recall you saying yesterday that Rose had a reputation for being a bit dramatic and unstable. Were you just upset at the time?"

"Yes, of course I was upset. But what I said was true. I asked around a bit before I hired her, and there were some people who claimed she was intrusive. She had been caught poking through someone's pantry, and another time was caught wandering through their house instead of staying in the living room. It was all enough to almost put me off her, but I decided to give her a chance. She did my reading for me, and it was amazing. We met at a coffee house so I wouldn't have to worry about her being nosy. But then, she and I got to know each other, and I really found it hard to believe that anyone could think of her that way. She was a kind person." Her chin trembled as she clutched the tea cup tightly in one hand. "Very kind."

"I'm so sorry, Betty." He gazed into her eyes. "I shouldn't have brought so much up."

"It's okay. Honestly, I have no one else to talk to about her. No one here knew her but me. I feel like everyone is just treating this like some kind of circus, instead of realizing that this was a real person, a human being, who was killed, right here in our own safe community."

"If you ever want to talk, I'm always available." Walt collected her empty cup and carried it to the sink. He washed it for her, then set it on the counter to dry.

"Thank you for your time, Walt, and thank you for checking on me." She walked him to the door. "I do hope that the police find the killer. That poor, dear woman. She may have had her faults, but she certainly didn't deserve this."

"I agree." He straightened his collar as he stepped out the door. He had some questions for his friend, Gerardo.

CHAPTER 7

*A*s Samantha parked her car in front of the coffee shop, she noticed that Jo was still silent in the passenger seat. Jo tended to be a quiet person, unless she was drawn into a heated debate, but it was unusual for her to be completely silent.

"Jo, is everything all right?" Samantha turned the car off and pulled the key out of the ignition.

"Yes, sorry." She wrung her hands, then frowned. "Actually, no. I'm a little worried about Walt going off on his own to talk to Betty."

"Jealous?" Samantha arched a brow and smiled.

"Hush." Jo rolled her eyes. "No, that's not what I mean. I'm just concerned that after all he's been through today, being in a strange house with a woman who is practically a stranger will be too much for him to handle."

"Walt has his quirks, but he is far stronger than we give him credit for. You should give him more benefit of the doubt. He can handle himself."

"I'm sure he can." Jo opened her door. "But should he have to?"

"I don't think that's up to us to decide. He didn't ask either of us to come along, did he?" She held open the door to the coffee shop for her. "Our little Walt is growing up, we have to give him the room to do just that."

"Yes, you're right." She sighed. "How did I end up being so overprotective?"

"It comes with the territory when you care about someone, I'm afraid." Samantha smiled as she led the way to an empty table. It was the last empty one available. The coffee shop was teeming with customers, and Samantha suspected that the food wasn't the reason they were there. Instead she guessed they'd all rushed to the coffee shop to discuss what happened in the empty villa. Which was exactly what they had hoped for.

"Afternoon ladies." Nancy, a waitress they were familiar with, leaned against the side of their table. She was usually quite peppy, but at the moment her hair was frizzed, her forehead was beaded with sweat, and she looked exhausted. "What can I get for you?"

"A little crazy in here today, hmm?" Samantha smiled at her.

"Yes, too crazy. Ever since the police rolled into Sage Gardens, this place has been packed."

"Oh, then you heard?" Samantha glanced over the menu in her hand.

"Yes, I did, I've heard it about one thousand times. I feel bad for the poor woman, but these aching feet just want to go home."

"I can understand that. We won't keep you." They both ordered soup and sandwiches. After Nancy walked away, Samantha looked over at Jo. "News does spread fast around here, but that's what we were counting on."

"Yes, it is, and look." Jo pointed towards a small group of people at the coffee bar. "I'm pretty sure I saw them yesterday morning, when we went for our readings."

"Perfect. I'm going to go say hello." Samantha left the table, and walked up to the coffee bar. A hush fell over the group as she paused beside them. She guessed that they knew about Walt discovering Rose's body.

"Afternoon." She smiled at them.

"Afternoon." A woman nodded in return. Samantha recognized her as Amy, a shy woman who she often spotted in her garden. "I'm curious about something."

"Yes?" Amy stared at her.

"Did you have a tea leaf reading done yesterday?"

"No." She looked at her friends, then back at Samantha. "None of us did. Dale went first."

"Oh." Her eyes widened. "So, he was the only one to get a reading?"

"Yes." Amy shrugged. "After that everything was canceled."

"I see." She sighed. "Thanks."

"Samantha, wait." Amy met her eyes. "Is it true? About Walt? Did he really kill her?"

"What?" Samantha laughed. "Are you kidding?"

"No." Amy's face grew pale. "We don't want to live near a murderer."

"Amy, Walt would never harm anyone. He had nothing to do with Rose's death. Please make sure you put that rumor to rest." Samantha did her best to hold back her frustration.

"Yes, I will." She nodded. "Sorry that I asked."

"It's all right." Samantha walked back towards the table with a knot in her stomach. It was not all right, not at all. "Nothing." She shook her head as she sat down with Jo. "There were no readings before Dale's."

"Too bad." Jo frowned. "We might still overhear something."

They both began to listen in to the conversations around them. To not appear too obvious, they fiddled with their phones. Samantha tuned in to a lively group seated just behind her.

"It's clearly a case of demonic murder." The high-pitched voice belonged to a woman named Ethel who was always asking invasive questions about religion and faith. "I've said it before, and I'll say it again, psychics are playing with fire, and in this case this poor woman was burned. I hate to say it, but she got what she asked for."

"Ethel, that's a little extreme don't you think?" The man beside her cringed as if he expected to be attacked.

"Extreme? Isn't it extreme to commit such a sin? I can show you right in the bible where it says…"

"All right, enough." Alice, a woman that Samantha knew from the decorating committee waved her hand through the air. "There was no demon involved here. It was a human hand that killed her."

"Then she awakened the evil in someone." Ethel shrugged. "It's as simple as that."

Samantha rolled her eyes. She didn't agree with Ethel's sentiment. However, she did make a note that Ethel might just be upset enough by Rose's presence in Sage Gardens that she could have wanted to cause the woman harm. It was an unlikely scenario but one worth considering. She glanced across the table at Jo and noticed that she had her ear tilted towards the next table over. Only two men were seated there with cups of coffee left to get cold in front of them.

"A woman in that line of work, she probably had a history with someone somewhere." The first man spoke in a slow drawl. He was from somewhere far enough in the south to practically have its own language. He pushed his coffee cup back and forth on the table but did not pick it up to take a drink.

"She was hiding things, Charles, that much I know." The man across from him, tall and thin to the point of appearing sickly hung his head. "I hate to see anyone killed, but I have to say, it doesn't surprise me."

"Well, there you have it, Rex. I don't suppose you could have done anything to stop it."

"No, nothing." He stood up from the table and tossed down a few dollars. "I guess, it is what it is."

~

*E*ddy did his best to distract himself. However, the more notes he jotted down, the more impatient he became. It was hard not to think about the plethora of information he could get from Detective Weiss. Still, he plodded through the details of what he'd discovered so far. Dale clearly had the kind of history that would make him a main suspect. However, the fact that he had been acquitted made everything difficult. Could he have been innocent of his wife's murder? If so, why was he accused in the first place? As far as he could tell her murder had never been solved.

Eddy looked up from his notepad as his phone chimed with a text. He saw that it was from Samantha. She invited him to join her at her villa that night for dinner and to discuss any leads in the case. He returned the text that he would be there, however he was a little disappointed that he wouldn't have much to share. All he knew was that Dale had been accused of murder in the past. That didn't make him Rose's killer. Also, he was acquitted, so it was likely that he hadn't committed the crime. Just as he set his phone back down it began to ring. He answered it right away, anticipating that it was Samantha.

"I just texted you back, Sam."

"Sam? This is James Weiss."

"Detective Weiss?" Eddy winced. "I'm so sorry, still getting used to these phones."

"Oh, trust me, I understand. I haven't been a detective for quite some time, but if you want to call me that, go right ahead."

"Once a cop, always a cop, right?"

"Right, so true. I hear you're retired, too. Eddy, is it?"

"Yes, Eddy is fine. Can I ask you a few questions about a case you investigated?"

"Sure, Marla told me it was about the Rice Murder."

"The Rice Murder?"

"Trust me, it sticks out in your mind once you've seen someone killed that way."

"What way exactly?"

"Before we dive into all of this, I need to know why you're asking questions about the case. Some of the information we kept under wraps, hoping that it would help us catch the killer."

"I understand. There was recently, as of this

morning, a murder in the retirement community that I live in. Now, one of the last people to have contact with this woman was your suspect, Dale. I can see in his file that he was acquitted, but I know that doesn't always equate to innocence."

"Especially not in his case. I was certain that Dale was the murderer, I just couldn't prove it."

"Why not?"

"Well, he had an alibi for the time of the crime. It was weak, but it was enough. He was a truck driver, and a worker at a local truck stop swore that Dale was there throughout the window of time in which the murder took place. However, there was no video to prove he was there, no financial record, no solid evidence other than the man's claim that he was there."

"That's very weak."

"I know, but I also couldn't find any evidence to prove that he was at the scene of the crime. Add to that, no history of violence, and no indication that he knew about his wife's affair and we have a very flimsy case. I pushed for it to go to trial against the DA's advice. I'm still buying him drinks to make up for that."

"Ouch." Eddy frowned as he made another note

on his notepad. "But you liked him for it, any particular reason why?"

"To begin with, the wife was killed by having rice poured down her throat which she choked on."

"What?" Eddy dropped his pencil.

"I know, it's shocking. It was shocking to those of us who saw it, too."

"I'm sure. But it's shocking to me, because the woman who was killed here, was killed in a very similar way. She choked on dry tea leaves."

"Wow! That is surprising. And you say Dale lives there as well?"

"Yes, he's my neighbor."

"Hmm, I'd be very cautious then. Was it his wife that he killed?"

"No, as far as I know he'd only met her once. He was quite angry with her, but he didn't know her personally."

"Well, that's odd. One of the reasons I was sure that Dale was the murderer in my case, was because the crime was so obviously personal. The rice indicated marriage to me, you know, they like to toss it at weddings. She'd been cheating on him for a few months. My theory was he found out, and he used the rice to make a point about their marriage being ruined. However, he claimed he knew nothing about the affair, and we couldn't find any evidence to indicate that he did. So, it was another dead end. The trial went nowhere, and Dale was set free within hours. The memory of him walking away from the courthouse still leaves me unsettled. I wish I had done more."

"You did what you could with what you had."

"Thanks. Just keep in mind, even though the crimes are similar, the motive sounds very different. Don't just assume Dale is the killer. Don't repeat my mistake, make sure you have real, solid evidence."

"I will. Thanks for the information." Eddy hung up the phone as his head spun. It didn't seem possible that Dale could be innocent of both his wife's murder and Rose's. The similarities of the two crimes were too blatant to ignore. One woman choked by rice, another woman choked by dry tea leaves. It isn't exactly a common way to kill someone. But the question on Eddy's mind was, how could he prove it? If Detective Weiss hadn't been able to prove that Dale killed his cheating wife, then how was he going to prove that Dale killed a perfect stranger?

alt headed to his favorite tea shop, called 'Tea'd Off'. He visited four times before he understood the name. Once he did, he chuckled to himself every time he drove up. He arrived just a few minutes before closing time. This was something he never did, as he did not believe in causing stress if it could be avoided. This evening however, he didn't think that it could be avoided. He didn't want to wait another day to discuss things with Gerardo. He hurried up to the door and stepped inside. The aroma of an assortment of teas slapped him in the face as it always did. For an instant, he got a bit of a headache as he tried to count the number of scents as well as classify each particular scent. After a few seconds, as always, the headache faded and he relaxed in the familiar environment.

"Gerardo?" He peered through the many shelves of boxes of tea.

"I'm back here, Walt!" His lightly accented voice wafted to him, right along with the scents of the shop. "You're awfully late today." He arched a thick brown eyebrow as he looked across a stack of boxes at him. "I hope you don't mind, I was getting a head start on my inventory."

"No, I don't mind." He fought the urge to point out that Gerardo had stacked his boxes in uneven piles, and that they were all in danger of toppling over. "I won't be here long, I promise."

"No problem. I have some fresh tea for you if you're ready for more, but I didn't think you would be yet."

"No, not just yet. However, I've come across two people recently who also had the same kind of fruit tea."

"Oh yes, it's becoming quite popular. It might have something to do with me recommending it, but it might also have to do with the upper class getting a taste of it."

"The upper class?" Walt eyed him with interest. "Who might that be?"

"I've had orders come from as far as Bright Bay Heights. It shocked me, but hey, if they're willing to pay the delivery charge I will take it out to them. You know how it goes, once one person in that crowd likes something it becomes trendy, so there's a good chance that tea will be in high demand soon. You might want to stock up on it." He winked, then turned back to his boxes. "So, if you're not here for tea, what can I help you with?"

"A little information." Walt pushed his glasses up along his nose and did his best to speak in a gentle tone. "I'm afraid, there was a murder at Sage Gardens."

"Rose?" He didn't turn back to look at Walt, but his shoulders tensed and his voice grew thick with emotion.

"Yes, you heard?" Walt shuffled from one foot to the other.

"I'd heard some chatter. But I was hoping that it wasn't true." He turned back to face Walt. His entire face had transformed with an emotion that Walt couldn't quite discern.

"I'm so sorry. I'm afraid it is true. Did you know her well?" He felt terrible for pressing the man, as he was clearly impacted by the news.

"Not very, no." He cleared his throat. "Walt, I'm

sorry but I will be closing soon, so if there's nothing else I can help you with…"

"I'm the one that found her, Gerardo." He stared into his eyes. "This morning."

He cleared his throat again, and Walt noticed right away that his lips were tight under his handlebar mustache.

"That's terrible, Walt." His voice wavered. "What a tragedy."

"It was, yes." Walt narrowed his eyes. "Betty told me that you recommended Rose to her. How could you do that if you didn't know her?"

"Lots of people frequent my shop. Rose asked me to let her know if anyone inquired about tea leaf readings. I thought she was clever to ask me about it, so I agreed. She seemed like a nice enough person, not the scam artist type. I guess, I just thought she could use a helping hand. I figured it couldn't hurt and might even bring in some new customers."

"Was she in some financial trouble, is that why you thought she needed some help?" Walt searched his expression for any sign of deceit. A quiver of his eyebrow, or a squinting of his eyes, might just reveal that Gerardo was hiding something. But neither of those things occurred.

"Look, whatever she was dealing with in her life, it's the police's business now. Like I said, I didn't know her well, and I don't like to get involved in the rumor mill. Some things are better left unsaid." He looked up at the clock. "It's closing time now. You're going to have to move along." He turned back to his stack of boxes.

"Wait, just one more question please, Gerardo." Walt's heart began to pound. He didn't want to upset Gerardo, but he also sensed that the usually cheerful and well-mannered man was hiding something.

"What is it?" He clenched his jaw and glanced back at him.

"Did Rose ever mention where she lived? What town she was from?" Walt held his breath as he hoped that Gerardo would have at least that information.

"Sure. Dradford. That's why I figured she could use the help. People around there, don't make a lot of money, and nobody lives there that doesn't have to." He shrugged. "I just hope that my attempt at kindness didn't lead to her death." He lowered his eyes. "I'd hate to think that. I really have to get this inventory done, Walt." He gestured to the door. "Do come back when you need more tea, but don't wait too long, or all of the snobs might snatch it up."

"Thanks for the warning." Walt smiled at him. Gerardo returned the smile. Everything felt fine on the surface, but tense underneath. He turned and left the tea shop. As he got back into his car he couldn't help but wonder whether he'd ever feel calm in his favorite place again. Two things had been revealed to him about Gerardo, he was not a good liar, and he had quite a bias against the wealthy.

~

The din of the surrounding patrons did nothing to distract Jo from the words that Rex spoke. He seemed to know something about Rose that might help the investigation. She had to find out what it was. She saw her chance to get more information about to walk out the door. She couldn't let that happen. As Rex walked by her table, she made her move.

"Excuse me." Jo reached up and touched the curve of Rex's elbow. "Would you sit with us for a moment?" She met his eyes as she smiled and gestured to the empty chair beside her. "Please?"

"How can I deny two beautiful ladies?" He offered a smile that revealed a chipped tooth and an endearing dimple in his right cheek. "What can I help you with?" He sat down at the table with them.

"I couldn't help overhearing that you knew Rose. I'm sorry, I know this will sound very strange, but our friend is the one who found her." Jo started then looked at Samantha to continue. Jo felt that Samantha would be more comfortable and successful at getting information out of him.

"He's very upset, and we're trying to find out more about her, to maybe help him heal from the trauma." Samantha looked straight into his eyes. She always found that the best way to get someone to give up information, was to be as honest as possible. As long as they felt as if they were speaking to a trustworthy person they were far more likely to be responsive.

"Oh, wow. I'm sorry to hear that. I'm Rex." He offered his hand. "Rex Tucket. I run the Sleep Here Inn, out on Fifty, do you know it?"

"Yes, I do." Samantha smiled. "I've heard good things about it. Chocolates on the pillows and fresh coffee in the morning?"

"Well, I do try." He chuckled. "Who doesn't like a little candy? I'm glad you've heard good things.

Anyway, that's how I know Rose. I can't say I know too much about her. She stayed for a few nights, and barely made a peep when she was there. I'm used to my guests getting a little rowdy, but not Rose."

"She seemed like a kind person, though I never had the chance to properly meet her. I know you didn't know her well, but you did mention something about her past?" Samantha let her voice trail off. She didn't want him to feel interrogated.

"Look, I'm not normally one to pass on information about my guests. I try to respect their privacy, and to be honest it's not great advertising to admit that a woman who stayed at my inn was murdered." He glanced over his shoulder at the crowd in the coffee shop, then looked back at them. "The thing is, she seemed like a sweet, quiet lady, but to tell you the truth I don't think she was who she said she was."

"What?" Samantha leaned forward as her heart slammed against her chest. "How can you be sure?"

"I can't, but she paid cash and wouldn't give me any ID, a sure sign that someone's trying to hide something. When I said I needed some ID for the registration and a credit card to put on file she just offered me more money."

"And?"

"I accepted it. She stayed only five days instead of the eight she was booked in for. All of a sudden yesterday, she turned in her key and checked out."

"You didn't find that strange?" Jo eyed him. "That she would just take off like that?"

"Not really. It's happened before. Sometimes people stay as long as they can before they think I'll become too suspicious, or they run out of money and they just disappear."

"What did you do? Did you call the police?" Samantha made a note on her phone.

"No. She hadn't done anything wrong really. She paid her bill plus some, she left a good tip. I figured if she was trying to hide from something, maybe she had good reason, and it would be better to leave her alone."

"And you have no idea where she went after that?" Samantha searched his eyes.

"No, sorry. The police asked me that, too. And whether she'd had any visitors while she stayed there. I don't make a habit out of keeping track of my guest's visitors but as far as I know she didn't have any. To be honest any time I was there, she wasn't. I'm not sure what she was up to, but it seemed to take up a lot of her time." He shrugged. "I guess she was trying to hide something, or run from something."

"What makes you think she was trying to hide something?" Jo sat back in her chair.

"I've seen a few women over the years show up at my motel, some with kids. They check in under a fake name, because they don't want a husband or boyfriend to be able to track them down. But most of the time they tell me about it, and if they do, I let them stay and I make sure they are watched out for until they are ready to move on. I would've done the same for Rose, but she didn't tell me anything was wrong." He frowned. "Maybe if she had, she'd still be alive. I feel guilty about that, even though there was nothing I could have done. I didn't know she was in any danger."

"So, you think a spouse or boyfriend was trying to hurt Rose?" Samantha shook her head. "I hadn't even really considered that, but it makes sense."

"I don't know what she was hiding from exactly, all I know is that she was hiding." He shrugged. "I wish I could tell you more. I hope your friend is able to overcome this tragedy."

"Thank you." Samantha stared after him as he left the coffee shop.

"It seems to me that there was quite a bit more

to Rose than we realized." Jo tapped her fingertips against the table. "And it's looking more and more likely that she was a scammer after all."

"Do you think so? You don't think she was on the run from someone?"

"I think she might have been on the run, because she was a scammer. Maybe she pulled a con on someone and they tracked her down here. Or maybe she checked out early, so she left before they had the chance to. That's a big sign that she was up to no good."

"You're right, it is. But what if what Rex said is true? Maybe Rose had good reason to be hiding." She sat back in her chair. "She could have had a stalker, a boyfriend or an ex."

"Maybe, but that doesn't really add up. If she had a stalker why would she volunteer to do a full day of tea leaf readings in one place where he might find her. And why would she have returned to Sage Gardens instead of moving on to some place new to throw him off?"

"Yes, that's true. It doesn't add up. I've already invited Eddy and Walt to join me for dinner tonight at my villa. I figured we can all pool our information and get to the bottom of this."

"Great. But I hate to tell you, Samantha, I'm not

sure we're anywhere near the bottom. I think we might have just grazed the top."

"I'm afraid you might be right about that." As Samantha and Jo left the coffee shop, they discussed the information they'd found out. It was promising, but it wasn't enough. Samantha hoped that at dinner they would be able to figure something more out.

CHAPTER 9

By that evening Samantha was still feeling just as frustrated. She popped open the last box of Chinese food and set it in the middle of the table. Although she loved food, she preferred, and was better at, eating it than cooking it. So she placed an order and had it delivered. A knock on the front door signaled that her friends had begun to arrive.

"Come on in, I'm in the dining room." Samantha tossed some forks on the table and one pair of chopsticks for Jo.

"Hi Samantha." Walt stepped in and sniffed the air. "Ah, A-1 Wok's?" He smiled.

"Yes, I never go anywhere else." She grinned as he headed straight for the table. "Don't worry I got you your favorite, vegetables."

"Thank you! You're so thoughtful." Walt sighed with contentment as he settled at the table. The next knock on the door was easy to recognize. It was heavy, two quick solid raps.

"Come on in, Eddy!" She grabbed glasses from the cabinets and iced tea from the refrigerator.

As the front door swung open, Eddy's voice preceded him, as well as his tone. It was sharp, determined, and impatient.

"You keep wanting to dismiss the possibility that Rose was a genuine tea leaf reader, but I think it's an angle that we have to focus on. If we ignore it, then we might just miss out on some very important information."

Jo stepped in behind him and rolled her eyes when she knew that he wasn't looking in her direction. "Because, Eddy it's nearly impossible. You want to believe that she really saw something in that reading, but the truth is it was most likely a scam. If you fall for it, then it'll throw off our entire investigation."

"Hey, I'm not falling for anything," he snapped, then sighed. "Forget it, we can revisit it later."

"Well, Jo and I overheard some important information when we were at the coffee shop." Samantha gestured for them all to sit down at the table.

"According to the owner of Sleep Here Inn where Rose was staying, she didn't give him any ID or credit card."

"Interesting." Eddy raised an eyebrow and sat forward in his chair. "I wonder what that will lead to. Did the owner have anything else to say?"

"His theory was that she might be on the run from a disgruntled spouse. I'm thinking that she's more likely on the run from someone she scammed in the past. She might be quite new to tea leaf reading, but she could have been running a different kind of scam under another name." Jo tapped her fingertip on the table. "New name, new act."

"That's possible." Walt nodded.

"Sure, it's possible. But I'm pretty sure I've already found the killer." Eddy's revelation drew everyone's attention.

"You have?" Walt looked across the table at him with surprise. "Who?"

"I looked more into Dale, and it turns out he was on trial in the past for the murder of his wife, who choked on rice poured down her throat." He shook his head. "Sound familiar?"

"Oh, how strange." Samantha's eyes widened. "I had no idea that Dale was a murderer."

"Technically he's not. He was acquitted. He

doesn't have any criminal history beyond that accusation and since the case was dismissed, he is considered innocent." He grunted beneath his breath. "Sometimes the system doesn't work."

"So, you believe he killed his wife?" Jo picked up her chopsticks and dug into one of the boxes of Chinese food. "Are you sure about that?"

"Yes, without further information I am. She was cheating on him, he has no alibi, and the rice seemed like a personal jab at their failed marriage." Eddy nodded, then slurped up a noodle. "I'd say it's pretty obvious that he was the killer, there just wasn't enough evidence to prove it."

"I see." Walt dabbed his lips with a napkin. "As much as I want to agree with you, Eddy, I can't. It is a huge leap to assume that a man is guilty of not just one crime, but two."

"Oh my goodness, I bet that's what Rose saw in the tea leaves." Samantha set her fork down. "If she saw that Dale was a murderer maybe it scared her so much that she took off."

"Maybe." Walt nodded slowly. "But why wouldn't she have gone to the police?"

"The police are usually pretty dismissive of people who claim to solve crimes with psychic abilities. There are a few that make it through, but a very small number." Eddy slurped another noodle. "I know it's a leap, but I think it's an easy one to make. Maybe Rose freaking out over the reading just confirms it."

"But that still doesn't explain why Dale would want to kill Rose." Jo frowned. "If Dale was afraid that she knew the truth why would he risk killing her? Wouldn't he just end up in the same position that he was with his wife's death?"

"That's a good point." Walt stirred the vegetables in his box.

"It is, if you're dealing with an average person. But remember if we are to believe that Dale already killed once, then he is not your average person. He is already a murderer. Which means that he's proven that he's capable of allowing his emotions to become violent. It might not have been the smart thing to do, but he might not have been worried about what was smart at the time. We saw how he overreacted at the end of the reading. He could have been sent into a rage, and decided to take that rage out on Rose."

"If that's even her name." Jo lifted her eyebrows.

"Good point." Eddy cleared his throat. "If we don't even know who our victim is then we are going to have a hard time finding the killer. This much I can tell you, if it was Dale, which I still believe it was, then we are going to have to be very careful about proving it. He got away with murder once. We can't let that happen again."

"If he's the killer." Samantha dug into her food.

"It seems to me that Gerardo, the man who owns the tea shop, knows more than he's willing to say." Walt frowned. "I can't help but think the two are connected somehow."

"But how is the problem." Eddy sighed. "As far as we know Gerardo hardly knew Rose, right?"

"So, he says." Jo took another bite of her food.

"It seems to me that everyone around Rose, including Rose, had something to hide. Even Betty, something just feels off about her." Samantha shook her head. "I wonder what kind of life Rose lived. She had to have a family, friends, out there some-where. I wonder if they even know that she's gone."

"The medical examiner will find out her true identity when he runs her fingerprints through the system." Eddy finished the last bite of his food. "That will at least give us a place to start. I'm also going to speak to the detective that's working the case. I think it's Brunner. If it is, he might be able to give me some information about the case, plus I want to warn him that Dale might be looking to skip town."

"Yes, those boxes on his porch were there for a reason." Samantha frowned. "I think I'll follow Betty in the morning. I want to know what she's really up to."

"You really think she's keeping secrets, huh?" Eddy eyed her for a moment.

"I do, and my mind won't rest about it until I find out one way or the other."

"That's the same way I feel about Gerardo right now. I know he's keeping something from me." Walt rubbed his hands together. "I just can't figure out what it is."

"If we're really curious about what Gerardo might be hiding, I could always take a peek inside the tea shop." Jo sat back and crossed one leg over the other. "It would be a simple in and out."

"Absolutely not." Walt locked eyes with Jo. "There's no reason to break in."

"Well, there might be." Eddy rubbed his chin. "Gerardo is the main connection between Rose and

Betty that we know of. If he knows more than he's saying, then we should find out what it is."

"Like I said, it won't take me long, it would be an easy job." Jo offered a casual shrug as if she were discussing some yard clean-up.

"Only if I come with you." Walt set down his glass of tea and looked across the table at her.

"You want to come with me?" She stared back at him. "I work alone."

"Not this time you don't. I know that shop better than anyone else, and I will be an asset to you." He held her gaze.

"Why do you want to come at all?"

"Because that shop is one of my favorite places to go. I don't want you causing any damage to it. I can make sure everything stays in place and that things go as smoothly as you claim they will."

"I don't need any assistance." Jo arched an eyebrow. "Or permission."

"All right now." Eddy rapped his knuckles on the table. "We're not going to get anywhere by squabbling. Jo, it might not be a bad idea to have Walt with you, if he knows the shop as well as he claims."

"Eddy has a good point, and you know how hard it is for him to encourage any kind of break-in." Samantha patted Jo's hand. "It doesn't hurt to have some backup."

"Uh, sometimes it does." Jo frowned. "Fine, I guess. We'll see how it goes." She smiled at Walt. "If I must have a partner, I guess you wouldn't be the worst one to have."

"Thank you." Walt smiled in return. If there was any tension in their argument it faded as quickly as it arose.

"Thanks for dinner, Samantha." Jo nodded to her, then headed for the door.

"I'll walk with you." Walt stood up from the table and headed after her. "Good night, Eddy, Samantha." He tipped his head towards them.

"Good night," Samantha called to them as she stood up from the table as well.

"Mind if I stick around to help you clean up?" Eddy gathered a few of the empty boxes from the table.

"There's not much to clean up." Samantha picked up the forks. "But you're always welcome to stay, Eddy." She smiled at him as he walked past her to the trashcan. "Is something on your mind?"

"I'm wondering if we should call the break-in off." He turned and leaned against the counter as she began to wash the few dishes left behind from dinner. "I'm not sure it's a good idea."

"Well, Jo is good at what she does, I'm sure she'll keep Walt safe." She added a bit more water to the dishpan. "Is that what you're worried about?"

"I don't know." He sighed and pressed his fingertips against his forehead. "You know that it goes against my nature for anyone to be involved in a crime. Jo only uses her skills for good now, but they're still breaking the law the moment they break into the shop."

"So, you're morally against it? I can understand that, but it's not as if they are going to steal anything or destroy property. It's about the same as a search warrant, don't you think?" She finished the dishes and dried her hands on a towel.

"No, I don't think so. A search warrant is authorized by a judge who has weighed the evidence and decided there is sufficient reason to invade someone's privacy."

"Okay, okay." She held up her hands. "I get your point. But following the system is what let Dale get away with murder in the first place, isn't it?" She met his eyes.

"Maybe." He gazed back at her for a long moment. "That's not so much what I'm concerned about. I'm more worried about what will happen if they get caught."

"They won't get caught." Samantha patted his hand. "If there's one thing we can count on it's Jo's skill, and if there's another thing we can count on it's Walt's caution. I know how difficult it is for you, Eddy, but if it leads to Rose's killer I think it is worth it."

"You may be right about that. Still, it leaves me unsettled."

"It's such a beautiful night, let's go out on the back porch. The stars are calling to me."

"Hm." He eyed her. "Or you're just trying to change the subject."

"Actually, I am." She grinned as she led him outside. "Because I'd rather talk about who Rose might actually be."

"Hopefully by tomorrow I'll find out. But honestly, it shouldn't take that long for the police to figure it out. They're going to find her true identity fairly quickly. The question is whether they will share that information with us." He shrugged. "Maybe they will."

"Let's hope." She leaned against the railing and looked up at the stars. Eddy leaned beside her. "I hope it gets solved fast."

"Me too. Sage Gardens can be such a peaceful place." He smiled a little as he stared at the same stars she did. "I remember when I first moved here, I thought I was going to be bored to tears. And for a little while I was, until I met you, and Walt, and Jo. But now I find myself feeling very protective of our quiet community."

"I know exactly what you mean. Whoever did this committed murder, but the murderer also stole something from all of us, a sense of peace and safety."

"At least from those of us that still believe in it." He looked at her. "I think both of us have seen too much to ever think that any place could ever actually be completely safe."

"Yes, you're right about that." Her expression clouded as she recalled some of the things she'd written about over the years. "But I do still believe in the truth, and justice."

"Me too, Samantha, me too." He patted her shoulder. "I should get going. I have some calls I can make tonight."

"Okay." She smiled at him. "Good night, Eddy."

"Good night, Samantha." He headed down the back steps to walk around to the front, but paused at the bottom. "Make sure you lock up, all right?"

"I always do." She waved to him as he walked away. As much as she hated to admit it, Eddy was right. She'd never have the same expectation of safety that others who lived in Sage Gardens did, but she wanted them to be able to keep that expectation.

CHAPTER 10

*W*alt waited for Jo to descend the steps, then followed after her.

"I hope that you aren't upset with me about all of that back there." He matched his pace to hers.

"Not at all. You make a reasonable argument."

"Thank you." He smiled. "I would never interfere if I didn't think it would be of benefit."

"I understand. But you don't have to walk me home, Walt." She glanced over at him. "I've been walking myself home for decades."

"And I imagine that you prefer it that way." He met her eyes and smiled.

"In most cases, yes, though it's nice to have certain company." She nudged him in the side with her elbow. "You in particular."

"Thank you." He cast his gaze around the quiet sidewalks. "You can never be too careful when there is a killer on the loose. I know you can take care of yourself, Jo, but you can't blame me for wanting to make sure that you are safe."

"Can't I?" She tilted her head to the side as she looked at him. "I actually find it a little insulting."

"You do?" His eyes widened. "I certainly don't mean to insult you. If you felt that way, then why did you allow me to walk with you?"

"Because I wanted to make sure that you got home safe." She grinned.

"Oh, I see." He laughed and shook his head. "You're always one step ahead of me, Jo."

"Speaking of which, if we're really going to do this break-in together, there are some rules that you're going to have to follow." She stopped in the middle of the sidewalk and turned to look at him. "No exceptions."

"I know all about your rules." He waved his hand. "I'll be good I promise."

"I'm serious, Walt." She looked into his eyes. "Every single time you break in somewhere there are huge risks that you face. Will there be someone inside with a gun? Will there be a silent alarm that will summon the police? Will there be a guard dog ready to protect their territory?"

"Oh, yes." He cleared his throat. "All of that sounds pretty intimidating."

"It is, it should be." She rested her hand on his shoulder and continued to hold his gaze. "These are just a few of the things that can go wrong, and no I don't expect them to happen, but I always have to be prepared for the possibility."

"I get it." He nodded as his expression grew more solemn. "Thanks for the reminder."

"There's more." She tightened her grasp on his shoulder and continued to stare into his eyes. "You have to do what I say, the moment I say it, without question. Understand?"

"Yes." He searched her eyes. "Jo, I trust you, don't you know that?"

"It's hard to believe." She dropped her hand back to her side. "I know with my past you probably wonder if I'm trustworthy. You're a great friend to me, Walt, but you're also quite logical, and logical probably causes you to doubt me."

"No, I don't doubt you. I know about your past, yes, at least what you've been willing to share with me. And I know who you are, right now, standing in front of me. I trust you, Jo." He smiled as he studied her. "That's never going to change."

"I hope not." She started to walk again. "So, we'll plan for tomorrow night, it needs to be late and…"

"Tomorrow night?" Walt hurried to catch up with her. "Why not tonight?"

"Tonight?" She looked over at him with wide eyes. "No, we need time to plan, time to go over the blueprint and…"

"I know that place inside and out. It's one of my favorite places to go. I've counted the steps it takes to get from the front door to the counter, from the counter to my favorite teas, to the bathroom, to the back room. In case you haven't noticed, counting is kind of my thing. If we wait another day, it might give Gerardo time to hide whatever evidence there might be of his connection to Rose." The urgency in his voice caused it to sound a little deeper than usual.

"Walt, are you okay?" Jo raised an eyebrow. "You're pretty wound up about this, aren't you?"

"Yes, of course I am. 'Tea'd Off' is like a sanctuary for me. If it's run by a killer, or someone associated with a killer, I need to know." His cheeks flushed. "Yes, I'm wound up. Until I find out the truth, I'm going to be all twisted up inside."

"I get it." She took his hand. "Just take a deep breath. Real slow." She met his eyes as his chest rose and fell. "Good, and another."

"Thanks." He followed her instructions. "Sorry about that."

"No need to apologize. I understand how you feel. Until this is all settled none of us are going to feel at ease. And you're right, the best time to strike would be tonight, before Gerardo figures out what to do next. I'll meet you at your place at ten tonight, all right?"

"Sure, yes, I'll be there." He smiled at her. "Thanks, Jo."

"For putting you in danger?" She laughed. "I'm not sure that you should thank me for that."

"For trusting me enough to let me be part of this." He gave her hand a squeeze. "It means a lot to me."

"It should." She winked at him. "There aren't too many I'd take along for the ride."

He watched as she walked the remainder of the distance to her villa. Once he was sure she was inside, he turned and headed down the path to his villa. Now that the plan had been made, that twist in his stomach turned into an entire swarm of butter-flies, eager to get out. It meant a lot to him that Jo trusted him, but would he be able to pull it off?

~

On his way home, Eddy thought about the moments he shared with Samantha. She was always so patient with him, no matter how gruff or difficult he became. There seemed to be a part of her that understood him on a much deeper level. He often felt as if he couldn't keep up with her level of courage and determination, but she always drew the best out of him. She also helped him find clarity when his mind was cluttered. Their conversation that evening reminded him that he didn't have to color within the lines anymore. Sure, he missed wearing a badge, but not wearing it meant he had a little more leeway when it came to investigating a case. If the detective on the case was willing to let him have some insight, then who was he to turn down that information? The curiosity about who Rose might really be threatened to drive him mad.

Once Eddy was settled in at home, he placed a call to the detective working the current case. He was familiar with Detective Brunner, and though at times he was rather brusque, he'd also expressed gratitude for the insight that Eddy provided on some of his cases. After a few rings, the young detective picked up.

"Hello, Detective Brunner." His tone was tight, as if he was annoyed that the phone dared to ring.

"Hi, it's Eddy. Do you have a minute?" Tension grew within him as he wondered if his goodwill had run out.

"What is it, Eddy? I'm working an active case, I don't have much time to spare."

"I know, that's why I'm calling." He leaned his elbow against his knee and felt the weight of the murder settle in on his shoulders. It was a familiar experience for him. Once he'd taken on a case as a police officer, or as a retiree, he wouldn't rest until it was solved. "I wanted to be sure that you had all of the information you needed about one of the suspects in the case, Dale."

"Dale? I know he had an argument with Rose during the tea leaf reading. Do you know something more than that?" His voice shifted. Eddy could hear the hunger in it. Clearly he didn't have too many leads on the case just yet.

"I looked into Dale's records, and found that he was accused of murder in the past."

"Yes, I know, he was accused of killing his wife. But he was acquitted. Did you think I wouldn't look into him?" The defensive tone made Eddy roll his eyes. Young cops of any kind always felt the need to prove themselves to the point that sometimes they were blinded by their own need for approval.

"Relax, I'm not calling your skills into question. I wouldn't be contacting you if I didn't think that you could figure this out. Now, do you want the information I have or not?"

"Sure. I guess so. I'm not sure how you could know anything I don't." He sighed.

"Do you know how his wife was killed?" Eddy heard the long pause on the phone.

"No, I couldn't find that information in the file. I tried to get in touch with the detective but I'm still waiting for his contact information."

"Well, I did speak to the detective. Detective Weiss. He's retired. He told me that Dale's wife was choked by rice poured down her throat. The same way that Rose was murdered with tea leaves. I don't see how that could be a coincidence. He also said that he believed Dale committed the crime, however there wasn't enough solid evidence to prove it. I think all of that points a finger pretty solidly in Dale's direction."

"Yes, it does." He took a deep breath. "I don't know how you do it, Eddy. Somehow you are always able to get good information."

"It's just experience, kid. You'll have more of it with every crime you solve. Now, listen. I don't want to step on your toes, but you need to know that Dale could be planning to move. My friend Samantha saw him piling boxes on his porch yesterday. If he takes off, you might lose your only opportunity to catch Rose's killer. This is not the time to drag your feet."

"I had no idea. I'm planning to get out there first thing in the morning to speak to him." He paused a moment, and when he spoke again, there was hesitation in his voice. "Do you want to join me?"

"Really?" Eddy tightened his grip on the phone and wondered if his hearing was failing him. "You want me to join you?"

"Yes, if you would be willing."

"Of course, I would."

"You'd have to be silent, and keep your distance, can I trust you to do that?"

"Sure, yes, of course you can." Eddy decided not to mention that he and Dale had almost gotten into a fistfight at the tea leaf reading. "Whatever I can do to help you, that's what I want to do."

"Great. I'm hoping your instincts or experience will help me to get the truth out of Dale. He seems like a slippery fellow, and I don't want to take any chances."

"He sure is slippery. I'd be happy to be there, and I'll follow your lead."

"Great. Around ten?"

"Sure. I can meet you there if you want. Dale's villa is a short walk from mine."

"Good. Just remember, you're there as my resource, not to conduct your own investigation. Got it?" His tone became stern.

"Got it, chief." Eddy did his best not to allow any hint of attitude into his tone. It was hard not to, since the young detective was still so green, but he knew that in his position, he would be saying the same thing. "Thanks for the opportunity."

"I hope it works out well. I'd love to get this case solved as quickly as possible. There's talk in the neighborhood about forming a security patrol. I can only imagine the amount of nuisance calls and disputes between residents that will flood the station."

"Oh yes, best to nip that in the bud." After Eddy hung up, he had to hold back a chuckle. As much as he believed in a community being proactive about safety, he could only imagine some of the characters that lived around him stalking the sidewalks at night. It would be funny in some ways, but dangerous in others. Fear could make people do things that they would never normally do. He'd seen some tragedies caused by good Samaritans with the best of intentions.

CHAPTER 11

*J*o walked up to Walt's villa as quietly as she could. At this late hour most of the residents were asleep, and those who weren't would be quite suspicious of anyone walking around. She didn't want to draw any extra attention. She put her foot on the bottom step of the porch, and Walt's door swung open.

"Don't worry I'm ready to go."

"Sh." She glanced over her shoulder, then back at him. "We have to be quiet."

"I know." He lowered his voice, then paused to make sure that his door was locked. As he joined her on the sidewalk he looked towards the road.

"Are we walking?"

"I left my car parked in the community parking lot earlier today so that no one would notice us leaving so late. You know the sound of a car driving by would have everyone at their windows."

"Yes, you're right. So clever." He smiled at her, then offered her his arm. "Shall we?"

"You know this isn't a night on the town, right?" She eyed him for a moment.

"That depends on whether you let me buy you dinner after."

"I knew this was a mistake." She started to walk down the sidewalk.

"Relax." He slipped his arm through hers. "I'm just trying to lighten the mood. Tension makes me nervous."

"It should make you nervous to break into a building. It could lead to both of us being in handcuffs. You need to recognize how serious this is." She shot a look in his direction.

"Jo, I recognize it. I've calculated the risk, estimated the potential for failure, and reassessed whether my involvement in this will benefit us or increase our risk. I've done the math, and now I've made my decision. There's no point to warning me about things I've already thought through in every possible way. So just try to relax. I'm here, and I'm involved, and I'm not going anywhere, no matter what you say." He tipped his head towards the parking lot. "The only factors I couldn't add in were whether you took the time to gas up the car, and your sometimes spotty driving skills."

"Sometimes spotty?" She narrowed her eyes. "I drive just fine."

"Sure, if you want to get pulled over." Walt rolled his eyes. "The speed limit is not a suggestion."

"And if you were to drive it would take us ten minutes to get out of the parking lot." She arched a brow.

"Mirror adjustment is important." Walt nodded, then waited for her to unlock the doors. "Let me get that for you." He reached for the driver's side door.

"No thanks, I can get my own door." She locked eyes with him.

"I'm sure you can, I was only trying to be courteous."

"Walt, I'm not the hold the door, pay the check, kind of woman. Got it?"

"Got it!" He cleared his throat and walked around to the other side of the car. After he wiped off the door handle, he climbed into the car. To his relief it was spotless. Whenever he rode in Samantha's car he had to detox after. The interior of Jo's car practically sparkled. "Did you just have it detailed?"

"Hmm?" She looked around the car. "Oh no, I wipe it down every time. Old habits, you know."

"Old habits?" He looked over at her. "What do you mean?"

"Not leaving any fingerprints behind." She started the engine.

"Ah right." He smiled some as he watched the way she observed everything around her. Jo was capable of taking in everything at once, while still looking as if she couldn't care less. He'd found over the length of their friendship that they actually shared a lot of similar compulsions, only she was much better at disguising them. "So, about the tea shop…"

"Oh sorry, not right now." She turned up the radio. "Before I work, I listen to music. It gets me in the right space."

"Okay." He settled back and let the music wash over him. It didn't take him long to figure out how the music helped. The high paced rhythm got his adrenaline pumping and the inane lyrics distracted him from any doubts that tried to creep into his mind. When they were a few blocks away from the tea shop, she turned off the music and took a deep breath.

"Now we wait." She parked on the street near

the shop, instead of in the empty parking lot beside it.

"Don't we want to be closer?"

"A car parked on the street means nothing, a car parked in an empty parking lot stands out." She winked at him. "Don't worry I'll have you trained before the night is over."

"Great. Then we can team up." He grinned.

"Oh really?" She laughed. "That would be interesting, but don't forget I'm retired."

"Yes of course." He glanced through the windshield. "So how long do we wait?"

"As long as it takes."

"It's dark. We can head in now. I know the place closes at nine today."

"Just wait." She rested her hand on his arm. "Patience."

"I'm all about patience, but this is just a waste of time, Jo." Walt shifted in his seat. "It's not good to sit still for too long."

"Remember the part about listening to me?" She cocked her head to the side and stared at him.

"Right." He released a long breath. "I'm listening."

"Good." She patted his knee. "Just because the tea shop is closed, that doesn't mean that all of the buildings are empty, too. The last thing we need is someone closing up shop and catching sight of us breaking in. That's where experience comes in. All right?" She glanced over at him. "Just take a few more deep breaths."

"Wait." He held up one hand.

"Walt, we've been over this, what I say goes!"

"Sh!" He held up his hand again.

"Excuse me?" Jo looked over at him with wide eyes. Walt was many things, but rude was not one of them.

"Listen." He leaned his head closer to the open car window.

"What is it?" Jo whispered as she leaned closer to him to listen as well.

"Voices." Walt closed his eyes for a moment, then nodded. "One of them belongs to Gerardo. I'm not sure about the other, but it sounds like a woman."

"I can barely hear them, how can you tell?"

"This is the part where you have to trust me, Jo." He flashed her a brief smile. "Perhaps we should get closer? I'm curious to know why Gerardo would still be here so late."

"Yes, let's get closer. Step out of the car very quietly." Jo led the way as she eased her door open and then shut again. Walt followed suit. Then he led the way towards the sound of the voices. At the corner of the shop he paused, and pointed down the alley between it and the store beside it.

"They're in the office. I can hear them more clearly now. It's definitely Gerardo, and the woman's voice is familiar. Very familiar. The office window is at the midpoint of the alley."

"Perfect. Let's get close enough to hear every word. We need all of the information that we can get." She was careful to muffle her steps as she approached the window. Walt followed behind her, as light on his feet as he could be. When they neared the window, he had to cover his mouth to stifle a gasp. He'd finally recognized the female voice.

"It's Betty," he whispered to Jo who crouched down below the window.

Jo listened to the voice for a moment, then she nodded, and placed her finger to her lips. As they remained silent, the voices of the pair wafted through the half-open window.

"In my place of business, Betty, they came in here and asked me about Rose. What was I supposed to say?" His voice grew more tense with every word he spoke.

"I don't know. The truth?" Betty laughed a little.

"That's what I want to know from you, Betty. The truth. What happened to her? Did you hurt her?" He growled.

"What? You're kidding right?" She laughed again. "Why would I do anything to hurt her?"

"Don't play ignorant. I know what you did, and Rose knew, too. She told me about it. Did she confront you about it? Is that why you killed her?"

Walt and Jo met eyes as the words floated above their heads.

"Keep quiet. I didn't kill anyone. Whatever you think you knew, or you ran your mouth about to Rose, is nonsense. I know you called her quite a few times. It will look like you had some kind of crush. I'm sure the police would be interested to hear about that. Did she tell you she wanted nothing to do with you? Is that why you went after her?"

"I only called her for one reason. Go ahead and tell the police, and then I will tell them how you are a thief. I'm sure they will be very interested in that. Do you really think they're going to believe anything that you say once I tell them the truth about you?"

Inside the office there was a loud bang. Jo started to stand up to peek in the window, but Walt grabbed her by the arm and tugged her back down.

He shook his head. She stared at him for a long moment, anxious that someone inside might be hurt.

"Real mature, Betty. What else are you going to break?"

"Listen, Gerardo, if I go down you go down, you just keep that in mind. Understand?"

"No one is going down. But Rose didn't deserve to die." His voice wavered some.

"No, she didn't. But her death has nothing to do with me." All of the anger faded out of Betty's voice. "She was a good woman, and a good friend to me. But there's nothing we can do about it now. And if I find out that you had something to do with it, Gerardo, I swear, it isn't the police that you will have to worry about."

"Keep threatening me, that's going to fix things. I should have turned you in the moment that Rose told me the truth. It was Rose that talked me out of it, did you know that?" His voice cracked. "She talked me out of it."

"Gerardo, you're losing your mind. If you did this, you need to tell the truth. The police might be able to work out a deal or something."

"I didn't do it. But I'm pretty sure I know who did." His voice hardened.

"Now you think I'm a murderer? I had nothing

to do with this. Look, the police already have a suspect. His name is Dale, and he looks good for it. Just try to relax until they lock him up."

"Relax? I don't think I'll ever be able to relax again. Go on, get out of here before I decide to pick up the phone and call the police."

"Just remember that call can work against you, too. Like it or not, we're in this together."

"I wish I'd never met you."

"Well you did, and there's no turning back now."

As a door slammed, Jo grabbed Walt's arm and pulled him close.

"We need to get out of here," she hissed, then guided him towards the street. Once they were back safely in the car, Jo started the engine.

"Well, we certainly learned some new things." Walt buckled his seat belt.

"Yes, we did." Jo pulled out on to the road. "Things I didn't expect."

"I don't know what to think." Walt sighed.

"I can't believe they were accusing each other of Rose's murder." Jo shook her head as she increased her speed. "And I couldn't figure out which one might be lying."

"Maybe neither of them is." He tugged the seat

belt away from his neck. "It's possible that they're both innocent."

"Of murder, maybe, but they're both guilty of something. He called Betty a thief? What did she steal? And she said that he was calling Rose the night before she died? What was that about?" She sped up a little more.

"I don't know, but we need to find out. I'm so disappointed in Gerardo. He acted as if he knew nothing about any of this. I thought he was a more honest man than that." He swallowed hard as she whipped around a turn. "Jo, maybe you should slow down a little."

"Oh sorry, I got caught up in my thoughts." She slowed down some. "It just sounded as if they both knew something about the other that they shouldn't. And yes, they both denied being involved in Rose's death, but who would confess to something like that? We need to find out what motive Gerardo and Betty could have had for murdering Rose."

"Well, Betty is more familiar with Sage Gardens, which makes her the more likely suspect."

"Yes, that's true, but Gerardo seemed to know more about what was going on with Rose. And, according to Betty he had a bit of a crush, or possibly an obsession with Rose. Maybe she denied him, and he couldn't take it."

"It's probably best if we wait to discuss all of this with Samantha and Eddy in the morning. Having four minds to work on it will help. We're both exhausted."

"That's for sure." She turned into Sage Gardens and drove towards Walt's villa.

"I'm a little disappointed I didn't get to break in anywhere with you." Walt smiled some.

"No, you're not." She laughed as she looked over at him. "You're relieved."

"Maybe. All right, yes, I am."

"It's okay, Walt. You still made a great partner." She watched as he walked up to the door, then waited until he was safely inside, before she drove away.

CHAPTER 12

Samantha woke the next morning with a thrill running through her veins. It had been a long time since she'd experienced that kind of adrenaline. After she had a light breakfast, she headed out to find out whatever she could about Betty. She'd had quite a bit of experience with stakeouts as a reporter, and even though she was a bit rusty, her old instincts were on high alert. The hardest part was waiting for Betty to get going. She lingered a few blocks away for almost an hour with no sign of movement from Betty's villa. A few minutes later she received a text from Jo.

Walt and I found out some interesting information last night. Can we meet to discuss?

Surprised that they had already done the break-in, she texted back.

On Betty's trail today, but can you fill me in?

The text that followed detailed a conversation between Betty and Gerardo that made her skin crawl. Just what was Betty up to? Hopefully she would find out something solid on her stakeout. She had to wait another hour before Betty finally emerged. When she did she headed straight for her car, then drove quickly out of the community. Samantha did her best to keep up without getting so close that Betty would notice the same car following behind her. After some time she realized they were headed into Dradford. Betty continued to drive until she reached a small antique shop. Its front window was filled with ornate houseware, vases, plates, trays, and other collectibles. Samantha continued to drive past the shop and parked a few blocks down. Then she counted a full sixty seconds before she stepped out of the car.

As she approached she watched for Betty. If she was caught now, any chance of finding out real information would be blown. She paused at the door of the shop and peered through the glass. Inside she could see Betty near the counter. There was no bell above the door, or any other sign of an alarm that would sound when she opened it. Her heart still fluttered when she pushed on the door and eased it open as quietly as she could. Once inside, she crept down one of the cluttered aisles. A large grandfather clock served as a perfect place for her to hide, but still see and hear the interaction between Betty and the man behind the counter. He was an older man, perhaps in his seventies, and quite fit for his age.

"What can I help you with?" His pleasant tone indicated years of customer service experience. "Is there something in particular you are looking for?"

"Actually, I'm interested in selling something." She lowered her voice so much that Samantha had to lean forward some to hear it. "Something that you couldn't sell here in your shop."

"I'm not sure I follow. If I wouldn't want to sell it in my shop then why are you asking me about it?"

"It's not the kind of thing you can sell off the shelf. I thought you might have some connections to someone who could help me out." She shrugged. "It might land you a nice finder's fee."

"Are you saying you're looking for a fence?" He sighed. "I'm not interested in anything like that."

"I'm not asking you to be. All I want to know, is if you know someone who is. I've got a great item to sell, but it's so hot that it will have to be handled with care."

"Nobody wants anything that hot." His tone grew impatient. "Like I said, I'm not interested."

"Look, I was told that you used to be interested in these kinds of things. I get it, you've changed your ways, and that's fine. All I'm asking for is a name, a phone number, just point me in the right direction, and I'll make it worth your while."

"I'm not in that game, I haven't been for years." He coughed, then shook his head. "You should go."

"I'm not going anywhere until you give me a name. It's that simple. Do you want me standing here talking about your past when the next rich and snooty customer comes in here to pick through this garbage?"

Samantha's eyes widened. She'd never heard Betty speak so harshly. It was like she was a completely different person.

"Fine, I'll give you a number. But I want nothing to do with any of this." He reached into a drawer under the counter, then looked back at her. "Listen to me, are you listening?"

"Yes, I'm all ears."

"This man, is a dangerous man. He was dangerous when I worked with him, and I can only imagine that he's even more dangerous now. You have to be careful."

"I will be." She snatched the piece of paper from his hand.

"Don't ever come back here. Do you understand me? I don't want any of this anywhere near my shop."

"Don't worry, I have no interest in anything you have to offer." She spun on her heel and walked towards the door.

"I'm sure you don't. You had a chance to do things differently, Betty, and you made the wrong choice." He chuckled. "I guess it runs in the family."

Betty stopped, and turned back to look at him.

"So you do know who I am?"

"Of course, I do."

"I have nothing to be ashamed of, unlike some other people I know. Just because you're all buttoned-up now, doesn't mean that your past disappears. It's going to come back to haunt you one day, and then we'll see who is so high and mighty."

"Just be careful, Betty. Maybe you think you're going down the right road, but it can lead you to some very dark, unexpected places. I've warned you enough, what happens from here on is your choice." He held his hands up in the air. "I wash my hands of all of it."

"I bet you do." She shook her head, then continued towards the door.

Samantha ducked down behind one of the statues and hoped that Betty wouldn't spot her. She was torn between following after her and attempting to ask the man behind the counter some questions. However, she knew that he was already pretty hot under the collar, and she could always come back and question him later. She decided that she would follow Betty to see where she headed next. Maybe she would overhear or see something that would give her definitive evidence of what Betty was trying to sell.

~

As Eddy prepared to leave to meet with Detective Brunner, his cell phone chimed with a text. He picked it up to check the message and saw that it was from Jo. She wanted to meet for breakfast to discuss what she and Walt found out the night before. He typed a quick message in return.

I have a meeting this morning. Can you send me an update?

Then he tucked his phone into his pocket and

headed out the door. As he walked towards Dale's villa, he could hear the sounds of the neighborhood emerging. Many were early risers, but in general people didn't leave the house until about nine unless there was a special event. That was when people would begin to work in their gardens, take their first stroll of the day, or head for the swimming pool. It was a gorgeous day with no hint of rain to come. Eddy didn't spare a thought for the sky, or the pool, or the good turn in the weather. All of his focus was on Dale. From what he knew of the man, he was a murderer, and if he could kill once, then he could very well kill again. He was also highly cunning. That made him far more dangerous, as he knew how to kill and get away with it. In his time as a police officer he had encountered some murders that involved spouses. It was always shocking to him that people could go from loving one another to murder. But then his marriage hadn't lasted long. Maybe if it had, he would have understood the kind of anger that could come with betrayal. He doubted it though. He paused a few feet away from Dale's villa to wait for Detective Brunner. He pulled up about a minute later.

"Morning Eddy." He stepped out of his car, an old rust-speckled thing that Eddy guessed he drove around because a detective's salary didn't cover anything fancy.

"Morning Detective Brunner. Thanks for the invite."

"Just remember what we agreed to. I am running this investigation, you are a fly on the wall, got it?"

"Yes sir." He gritted his teeth and tried not to think about how much younger Detective Brunner was than him. It didn't matter. He had the authority in the situation, and as he'd seen him handle a few cases before, the young detective had already earned his respect.

Detective Brunner led the way up the steps and on to Dale's porch. It was still cluttered with boxes, as Samantha had reported. He knocked on the door, and introduced himself when Dale opened it.

"Great, what do you want?" Dale glared out at him, then past him, at Eddy. "And what's he doing here?"

"Dale, I'm just here to ask you some questions, that's all." Detective Brunner met his eyes. "I don't want to cause you any trouble."

"Sure, you don't. So why are you here?"

Detective Brunner asked him the usual introductory questions about his whereabouts at the time of the murder, whether he'd heard or seen anything unusual, and if he knew Rose.

"I met her the day of the tea leaf readings."

"Oh, is that something you're usually interested in?" The detective made a note.

"No, not really. I just thought, maybe for once, someone would see the truth." He frowned. "So, I went to the reading, and right away I could tell that she was a fraud. Then she did her little theatrical reaction, and I knew."

"You knew what?" The detective studied him.

"I knew that she had done her research on me, that she knew about my past, and she was going to tell everyone about it." He shook his head. "That's why I've been packing up. It won't be long before I'm run out of here. I thought I'd finally found a place where I could live my life, but I was wrong. Now if you don't mind, I have a lot of packing to get done."

"Just a minute." Detective Brunner slipped his foot inside the door to stop Dale from closing it. "I'm not done."

"Of course not." He stepped back out and held out his hands, wrists up. "Go ahead, arrest me."

"I'm not here to arrest you, unless you feel you have something to confess."

"The only thing I have to confess is that I didn't kill my wife, or Rose! But it doesn't matter does it? It doesn't matter that all of the charges were dropped, in your eyes I'm still guilty."

"That's not the case. I'm just here to find out the truth. I've been told you were very upset with Rose after the reading. Was that the last time that you saw her?"

Eddy focused his attention on Dale. If he lied, he hoped he would be able to tell. He was getting a little rusty since he'd been retired, but he could usually pick out a lie.

"Yeah, I saw her again." He sighed and let his hands fall back to his sides. "But I didn't kill her."

"It's all right, just tell me about it. Maybe it will help us find the real killer."

Dale relaxed some, then shot a glare in Eddy's direction.

"I still don't know why he's here."

"He consults on cases for me now and then. There's nothing to worry about."

"He's a real hot head you know?" Dale rolled his eyes.

"Never mind that, when did you see Rose?"

"I went looking for her. I wanted to." He paused

and looked away. "I didn't want her telling everyone about my past. I really like it here."

"And did you find her?"

"Sure, that night. I found her. She and some guy were having an argument in the parking lot."

"Some guy?" The detective studied him. "What were they arguing about?"

"I'm not sure, I didn't get close enough to find out. But he was angry, and I figured that she'd scammed him, too. I didn't want to get in the middle of it, so I just left."

"That's it?" Eddy stepped forward. "You didn't even speak to her, even though you were so angry and desperate to shut her up?"

"Eddy." Detective Brunner shot him a look.

"I wasn't going to hurt her!" Dale nearly shouted his words. "I just wanted her to understand, I'm innocent, I didn't do anything to deserve this life! Do you know what it's like to be accused of murdering your own wife? People think you're a monster!"

"Aren't you?" Eddy stared him square in the eyes. "Didn't you feel just as betrayed by Rose as you were by your wife? One cheated on you, and the other was going to ruin your life?"

"You have no idea what you're talking about!"

Dale surged forward so fast that Detective Brunner didn't have time to get between them before Eddy was shoved half over the railing.

"Dale! Hands off!" Detective Brunner put his hand on the butt of his weapon. "I don't want to have to arrest you."

"Fine." Dale cleared his throat and straightened up. "I told you what you wanted to know. Now get off my porch!"

"Wait, what about the man she was talking to. Do you remember anything about him? What he looked like? Did she say his name?" Detective Brunner asked.

"She shouted it." He closed his eyes, as his chest still heaved with anger. "It was something a little strange. Uh, Jared, no Gerardo! It was Gerardo. Get him off my property or I will!" He pointed at Eddy.

"We're leaving, we're leaving now." Detective Brunner pointed down the steps. Eddy reluctantly followed his instructions. As they walked away from the villa he could feel Detective Brunner's disapproval.

"What happened to following my lead?" He frowned.

"I got you a name, didn't I?" Eddy offered a

half-smile. Then he lowered his head some. "I'm sorry I lost control there a little. I'm afraid I still slip into old habits."

"It's all right, Eddy. I have to admit, I invited you here just for that reason. I thought where I might be too weak, your strength might come through."

"You did a pretty good job, Detective. I'd be honored to work with you any time."

"I certainly have to do some digging into Gerardo. Let me know if you come up with anything."

"I will."

CHAPTER 13

*O*nce Betty returned to her car, Samantha watched her pull into the street. She drove with a sharpness, a bit more gas than needed, and a last minute jerk of the wheel. It was clear to her that she was upset. The conversation she'd just had touched a nerve. What Samantha gathered from it was that Betty had been involved in something illegal, and though she had the chance to escape it, she didn't. She was likely going to meet the dangerous man that the antique shop owner had referred her to. Even though she wasn't sure how Betty was involved in Rose's death, if at all, the thought of her going to meet a man like that all alone, made Samantha uneasy. At least she could be her backup if things got messy.

After giving Betty a little room for a head start,

she settled in a few car lengths behind her. They drove deeper into Dradford, all the way to the edge of it, where it met Bright Bay Heights. Betty finally pulled over into the parking lot of a high-end restaurant. Samantha was surprised when she drove past and saw that Betty had parked. Was she really going to meet a fence at such a fancy place? She parked in the next plaza, and walked over to the restaurant. As the hostess led her to a table she did her best to figure out where Betty was seated. At first she thought she'd lost her. The restaurant was fairly busy as it was close to lunch time, and most of the tables had three or more people seated at them. Samantha was the only solo diner, which she knew would make her stand out. Before the waitress could come over, she got up and headed to the bathroom. It was all the way in the back. As she neared it, she heard a familiar voice.

"I'm trying to find a solution here."

It was Betty. Samantha ducked behind a large fern and listened as the man she sat across from responded.

"The solution was to get rid of it when I told you to, years ago. That was the solution."

A quick look at the man across from Betty

revealed that he was at least twenty years her senior.

"The past doesn't matter now. We have to focus on where we are. I think this guy might be willing to buy it all."

"Or he might decide to turn you in. You can't trust him, Betty. You can't trust anyone. Have I taught you nothing?"

"Dad, I know that I shouldn't trust him. But I have to do something and fast."

Samantha's heart skipped a beat. The man at the table was Betty's father? And apparently he knew about whatever it was she had stolen and was trying to sell.

"Just get rid of it, all of it. Just dump it somewhere. That's what you should do."

"No way. I'm going to make sure you get what you deserve out of it, Dad."

"Excuse me?"

Samantha jumped at the sound of a voice behind her.

"Are you lost? Do you need help with something?" The young waitress eyed her with clear judgment.

"Sorry, I was just trying to tell what kind of fern this is, it's so beautiful."

"It's a fern. You know, the plant kind. Are you going to order?" She sniffed as if Samantha carried a very repulsive scent.

"Actually, I changed my mind." She hurried past the waitress and towards the door. She knew that at any moment Betty might catch sight of her, and if she did there would be no explaining how she could have ended up at the same restaurant two towns away. Just as she would lay eyes on her, Samantha ducked through a door and found herself in the kitchen. The kitchen staff didn't seem to notice her at first as they were all focused on their duties. She took a deep breath of the delicious scents that surrounded her and wished she had decided to stay for lunch after all.

"What are you doing in here?" One of the chefs barked in her direction. "No guests in the kitchen!"

"I'm sorry, I just got turned around. I was looking for the restroom. It isn't through here?" She blinked and glanced around as if she'd never seen a kitchen before.

"No, it's not." He pointed at the door she'd step through. "Out and to the left, then down the hall. Quickly please."

"Yes, of course, right away. So sorry for the interruption." As she stepped back through the door she could only hope that Betty was already gone. When the door was shoved shut behind her she was forced into the back of someone just outside the door. He turned to face her, and she recognized him right away. It was Betty's father.

"Excuse me, I'm so sorry." He stepped aside. "I didn't mean to block your way."

"It's quite all right, I shouldn't have been in there in the first place. I got lost."

"This place can be a bit confusing." He chuckled. "Do you dine here often?"

"No, in fact, I never have. I'm on my way out." She spared him a smile. "Have a good day."

"Oh dear, wait a moment, are you really going to miss the food they have to offer here?" His eyes widened with horror.

"I'm afraid it's not in my budget. I was passing by and noticed it, and thought I might enjoy it, but it's not quite my kind of place."

"I'm sure it could be." He offered her his hand. "Why don't you join me? I haven't finished my meal yet. It will be a treat for me to have some company, and my treat for you. How does that sound?"

She had the feeling that he was hoping for more than sharing a meal. Even well into his seventies or even early eighties the man had a charming nature that was impossible to ignore. But that was not what drew her to the table with him. It was the opportunity to learn more about Betty, and her father, and what they might have stolen. As she settled across from him, he smiled at her, and summoned the waitress. The same waitress she'd spoken to a few minutes before arrived at the table. She gave Samantha a strange look, then simply took her order. Once it was placed, Samantha looked back at the man across from her.

"Thank you for your kindness, Mr.?"

"Devlin. John Devlin. And you are?"

"Samantha." She smiled, with no intention of giving him her full name. "I saw you with a woman just now, are you sure I'm not interrupting?"

"Oh no, that's my daughter Elizabeth. She likes to check in with me now and then. But she's always busy with something."

"I understand. She seemed a little upset."

"She's still young. I've tried to explain to her that there's no point to taking anything that seriously, but she doesn't listen. She's caught up in proving herself. You know how that goes."

"I have an idea." She nodded.

They shared their meal as he entertained her

with tales of Elizabeth as a young girl and her determination.

"At times, I honestly thought she was obsessed. I worried about her. She was so focused on being a part of the family business that she refused to go to school, she never participated in things girls her age did. She had no interest in romance, only wealth." He chuckled. "I suppose it made me proud, it still does."

"That's a beautiful thing. It sounds like she's a real treasure."

"She is, in many ways." He finished his last bite of food. "Shall we have dessert?"

"No thank you, I really must be going. I've enjoyed this talk, Mr. Devlin."

"Please, call me John." He met her eyes. "You remind me of my Elizabeth in some ways. You have that same determined look in your eyes. Don't let it eat you alive. I should have taught my daughter that. Once she makes a decision, she sticks to it no matter what. I'm afraid it's sometimes to her detriment."

"I will keep that in mind, thank you." She smiled at him as she left the table. Though she was tempted to ask him more questions, she got the impression that he wouldn't reveal anything incriminating about his daughter and she didn't want to appear suspicious by asking too many questions. On the way out the door she received a text from Eddy requesting a meet-up at the coffee shop. She was stuffed, but she had a lot of information to share. She sent him a text back letting him know it would take her some time to get back into the area.

～

*W*hen Eddy received the text from Samantha he was surprised that she had gone so far out of town. He joined the others at the coffee shop, but they all agreed to wait to discuss things until Samantha arrived. The information that Detective Brunner had called him with was burning in his mind. He was certain it would lead them to the truth about the murder. When Samantha finally arrived, he spilled the words out before she could even greet everyone.

"Detective Brunner found out who Rose really was, and none of you are going to believe this." Eddy looked around the table at each of them.

"Who is she?" Walt sat forward.

"Some scam artist right?" Jo quirked a brow.

Eddy glanced around the coffee shop and didn't say a word.

"Eddy, don't keep us in suspense." Samantha frowned.

"Sorry, I just wanted to be sure that no one was close enough to hear me. As it turns out Rose, is actually Maryanne Marlin. The daughter of oil baron Edgar Marlin."

"What?" Samantha's eyes widened. "Why in the world would she be working as a tea leaf reader?"

"I'm guessing the family is wealthy? I've never heard of this Edgar Marlin." Jo glanced between the two of them.

"Yes, very wealthy." Eddy nodded. "Almost the wealthiest family in Bright Bay Heights."

"I don't understand. If the family is so wealthy what was Rose doing here?" Puzzled, Walt's eyes clouded over as he began doing calculations in his head. "She could have easily opened her own shop if she wanted to do readings. Why would she want the inconvenience of traveling around?"

"Let's not forget she was living under a different name. Maybe it was for her career as a tea leaf reader. Or maybe she was estranged from her family." Samantha looked back at Eddy. "Did you find anything else out?"

"Yes, mainly that she was not estranged from her family. She visited her father every week. He is in poor health and has nurses caring for him twenty-four hours a day. The family did maintain a fairly private lifestyle and didn't often socialize with others. At this point Detective Brunner has hit a brick wall. He can't explain how Maryanne became Rose or why." He sighed. "And neither can I. I've been running it through my head ever since I found out, but nothing I piece together makes sense to me."

"I still say if someone is using a different name they are either on the run or trying to hide from something. Was there ever any kind of scandal in the family?" Jo waved the waitress away as she approached. "Was there anything that she might have been ashamed of?"

"Not that I know of, but I haven't done any real research on the family yet. I wanted to share the information first and see what everyone thought."

"I can handle the research." Samantha pulled out her phone. "Even if the Marlins did keep a low profile, any kind of scandal in a wealthy family makes its way to the news or the gossip columns."

"While you do that, I think we should focus in on Gerardo. Again, he was the only one that we know of that had contact with Rose and Betty. He connected them. Dale claims that he saw Rose arguing with him the night she was killed. Now, it could be Dale's way of throwing us off his scent, but as far as I know he has no connection to Gerardo. I think Gerardo has some information we need. I'm just not sure how we can get it." Eddy frowned.

"We could try breaking in, we never went through with it the first time." Jo shrugged.

"You could, but I don't think this is the kind of information we're going to find just laying around. We need him to talk to someone he trusts," Eddy said.

All eyes at the table turned on Walt.

"You think he trusts me?" Walt raised his eyebrows.

"You're the best chance we've got." Eddy nodded. "You're the one that he knows out of all of us, and you've been there so frequently that he's quite familiar with you. He won't see you as a threat."

"I guess you're right. I'm just not sure I can get him to talk. My social graces are not exactly stellar."

"You'll do fine, Walt." Jo patted his hand. "It's just another puzzle to solve, right?"

"Right." He smiled, and relaxed. Jo knew how to put things into perspective for him.

"Anything I can do to help?" Jo met Eddy's eyes. For a split-second she saw a spark of interest, then it faded as he looked away.

"Not at the moment I don't think. Let's eat, hmm?" He gestured to the waitress to have her come take their orders. Throughout lunch Jo couldn't forget that spark in Eddy's eyes. She knew there was something he wanted her to do, but he didn't dare to say it. She could only guess what it was, but it wasn't hard to figure out. Betty was a thief or at least her father was and she had some kind of connection to Rose that they hadn't been able to establish. In order for the investigation to move forward they needed to know more about her. But the only way to find out, was to do some deep digging. She needed to get into Betty's villa and find out what she might be hiding. By the time they all went their separate ways, Jo knew exactly what she had to do.

CHAPTER 14

*a*s the four friends walked out of the coffee shop, Eddy held the door for Samantha.

"Thank you. You're such a gentleman." She winked at him.

"Don't let that get around." He grinned as he met her eyes. "What do you say we work together this afternoon?"

"That sounds good. Want to meet me at my place?"

"Sure, I'll be right behind you." He walked her to her car, then headed over to his own. Her mind focused in on what she might be able to find out about the Marlins. Wealthy families tended to have secrets, the only problem was they usually buried those secrets very well. If that was the case it might be hard to dig up anything. But her instincts told her that there was definitely something there for her to find. When she arrived at her villa, Eddy arrived right behind her. They walked in together, and as she set down her purse and keys, he started to make a plan.

"While you see if you can find out anything about the Marlins, I'm going to check the police database for anything hinky in Betty's past. Clearly, she's been involved in some kind of crime. Unfortunately, if she wasn't caught there might not be any record of it, but it doesn't hurt to look."

"That's a good idea, Eddy. Let me make some coffee, then I'll get down to it. If there is anything to find it won't take me long to find it."

"Great." Eddy settled in his favorite chair in Samantha's living room and closed his eyes for a moment. As he settled into a deeper rest his mind drifted back to the moment at the coffee shop when Jo asked if there was anything she could do to help. He did have an idea of something she could do, but he hadn't been able to say it. Could he really suggest criminal behavior? It made him uneasy to think of it. The chime of his cell phone startled him out of his thoughts. He looked down at his phone and discovered a message from Jo. It was a picture of a thumbs up. He stared at it for a long moment. Was it possible that she had figured out what he was thinking? His heart skipped a beat as he wondered if he should text her back and tell her not to do it, or question why she'd sent the symbol. If he did, she might tell him her plan, then he'd feel even more obligated to stop her. Instead, he turned the screen off and closed his eyes again.

"Do you want some milk in your coffee, Eddy?"

"No, thanks."

"Are you sure?"

"Yes, Samantha." He smiled as she brought him a mug of coffee. She asked him every time if he wanted milk, and he said no every time. She tried to soften his hard edges in so many ways.

"I don't know how you can drink it like that." She scrunched up her nose.

"It's gotten me through many late nights." He took a sip. "Excellent, thank you."

"You're welcome." She set up her computer on the coffee table and began to type away. "You said the Marlins are from Bright Bay Heights, right?"

"Yes, from what I understand they have quite a long history there."

"Okay good, that should make it easier to find out information. Let's see here." She scrolled down through several links, then paused when she came across one titled, 'Historical Treasures'. She clicked on the link and ended up on the website of the Bright Bay Heights Historical Museum. She skimmed through some information about the museum, then landed on the section that brought her there. There was a picture of a complete tea set, the cups didn't look particularly special to her, they were just white, but there were some photos of the underside of a cup, saucer and teapot. There was an intricate painting of a butterfly in gold.

"Eddy, listen to this. Until 1995 the Marlin family loaned this beautiful tea set to the museum for their annual tea party. It has been authenticated as the only surviving complete tea set and there were only five sets made. They were all hand-painted. The set has an elaborate hand painted design in gold. So, essentially it is one of a kind. Its history can be traced back to England and there are rumors that it may have once been owned by the Royal Family. After 1995 however, the Marlin family refused to loan it to the museum. Perhaps because of its value, or perhaps because Maryanne Marlin took over the day to day business of the family at that time. The Marlins have not given any kind of explanation for their refusal, and the museum is grateful to have enjoyed the presence of the tea set for the many years it was loaned to us."

"Interesting." He furrowed his eyebrow. "But that was over twenty years ago. Do you really think that could have anything to do with what is happening now?"

"Maybe Betty is involved with the museum somehow? Maybe she was upset that Maryanne refused to loan out the tea set?"

"Tea set." Eddy sighed. "Why is everything in this case coming back to tea?"

"I'm not sure. It seems funny though that Maryanne's family had this unique and valuable tea set, and then she was a tea leaf reader."

"All right let's consider what we know." He pressed his fingertips against his forehead. "Betty has been accused of being a thief, you overheard her trying to sell stolen merchandise, that perhaps her father stole."

"Wait a minute, Eddy, that could be it." Samantha's eyes widened.

"What do you mean?" He stared at her.

"Maybe the tea set was stolen. Maybe that's why they couldn't loan it to the museum anymore. Maybe that's why Betty was trying to get rid of it."

"Well, that's easy enough to check. I'm sure if it

was stolen they would have filed a police report. You say it was 1995?"

"Yes." She double-checked the date. "Betty's father would have been twenty years younger and more than capable of stealing, not that he wouldn't necessarily be now. He said that she was determined to be part of the family business. I can only guess he was referring to the business of stealing."

"Wait a minute, don't rush to judgment. Remember, we need solid proof. Assumptions are easily made, but not always true, and even if they are true, without proof to present in court they will likely dissolve."

"Right." She sighed. "So we need to find out if they stole the tea set, and if they did, why all of this came to a head now."

"Yes, we do." He frowned. "Which is not going to be an easy task. Even if we can connect the tea set to Betty, we still need to prove that she was the killer."

"If she was the killer." Samantha tapped her fingertips on a few keys. "Her father mentioned more than once that she seemed to be overly determined and obsessed. Maybe that drive was enough to turn her into a killer."

"Maybe." Eddy gazed over her shoulder at a

photograph of Betty and her father when they were both younger. "Like father like daughter?"

"It seems that way." Samantha nodded. As far as she could tell John Devlin was a thief, was he also a murderer?

~

*W*alt pushed open the door to his favorite tea shop and tried not to think about his plans to break into it the night before. He spotted Gerardo behind the counter and walked straight towards it. It was still the same number of footsteps from the door. While he worked as an accountant before he retired, his love of numbers had served him well, now, it sometimes drew the wrong kind of attention.

"Hi Walt." Gerardo glanced up from his phone. His cheeks were red, something that Walt rarely saw.

"Good afternoon, Gerardo. Is everything all right?" Walt rested his hands on the counter and studied the man intently.

"It's fine." He set his phone down, then cleared his throat. "It's still a bit soon for you to need more tea isn't it?"

"Yes, it is." Walt thought of all of the lies he could tell to try to sway Gerardo into confessing something, but he was such a terrible liar, he knew Gerardo would see right through him. "I'm here to see you, actually."

"Me?" His eyes narrowed. "Why?"

"Honestly Gerardo, I consider you a friend. I don't have many. I prefer it that way. But you have become someone I look forward to seeing each week when I replenish my supply. I hope that you might consider me a friend as well." He watched the man's expression, which grew a bit more relaxed.

"I do consider you a friend, Walt. I look forward to seeing you, too. But right now, I have a lot on my plate." He reached up and scratched the back of his neck. "Some things have come up that I have to deal with."

"Things that involve Maryanne?" He rushed the name past his lips as casually as he could.

"I barely knew her, like I told you before." He frowned.

"No, actually. You told me that you barely knew Rose. Not Maryanne." Walt smiled some. "So, you did know who she really was?"

"Yes, fine." He scowled at Walt. "Is this how you treat your friends?"

"If I can tell they're lying to me, then yes." He locked his eyes to Gerardo's. "Why don't you just tell me what happened? Did you have a fight with her? Did something go wrong?"

"I had nothing to do with her death, Walt." He turned his back to Walt and began shuffling through the boxes on the shelf behind the counter.

"You had something to do with it, or you wouldn't be carrying so much guilt. What really happened, Gerardo? How did you know Maryanne?" He pounded one fist against the counter. "Answer me, Gerardo, I can't help you unless you tell me the truth."

"I'm not asking for your help." Gerardo spun around so fast that Walt grew dizzy from the sudden movement. He grabbed the edge of the counter to steady himself. "What you need to do is stay out of this!"

"I can't." Walt swallowed hard as he stared at the man he thought he knew fairly well. "I was the one that found her. So no, I can't stay out of it. I want to know the truth. A father has been left without his daughter, and justice needs to be served."

"Walt, please, don't tell me anything more." He stepped back from the counter as the flush drained from his cheeks. "I don't know what happened to her, I don't want to know. I tried to do her a favor, and in some small way maybe I am responsible, but it wasn't by my hand."

"Then how? Did you know her as Maryanne?"

"Not at first." He sighed. "She came to me as Rose, and gave me this story about wanting to do tea leaf readings. But something about her reminded me of someone, so I did a little research on her, and it didn't take me long to discover that she was Maryanne Marlin. I knew her from the tea parties that the Bright Bay Heights Historical Museum used to host. I would supply the tea for it, and she would be there to showcase her family's tea set. But that was over twenty years ago. That's why I didn't recognize her right away. When I confronted her about it, she told me a story that was hard for me to believe."

"Oh? What story?" Walt focused his attention on every word that Gerardo spoke.

"She's gone now, I guess the truth is going to come out either way. She told me that the reason the family stopped loaning out the tea set was because it was stolen. They never reported the theft because they didn't want to appear vulnerable and they didn't want word to get out that it was on the black market. They were afraid that if it was sold or exchanged hands too many times they'd never get it back. Her father is ill, and one of his last wishes is to know what happened to the tea set. It was originally his late mother's and it holds great sentimental value. Maryanne had heard rumors that someone local still had the tea set. She had recently taken a course in tea leaf reading because she was interested in it and decided to come to the area to do some readings, immerse herself in the community in the hope that she may find the set. She said that she never believed that she would find it, but she had to try. She also asked me to tell her if I heard anyone mentioning a unique set, or an antique set. I am part of a tea paraphernalia collecting group. I told her she should just go to the police, but she felt the crime had been committed so long ago that it was pointless. This was the best that she could do. Not only would she have a chance at finding the set, but it would also give her a break from the business and some distraction from her father's ailing health."

"What a story." Walt shook his head. "What happened next? Did she find the tea set?"

"No, she didn't." Gerardo's expression hardened. "Not that I know of, anyway."

Walt stared at the man as he recalled him

accusing Betty of being a thief. Betty also threatened him in return. Was he trying to set Betty up to take the fall? He wasn't sure what to think, but he was almost certain that Gerardo knew exactly who had the tea set, which meant that he was still lying.

"Thank you for sharing all of that with me, Gerardo. I appreciate it." Walt frowned. "It sounds to me like a sad story just got sadder, however."

"Indeed." Gerardo closed his eyes, then looked at Walt again. "I never would have wanted her to get hurt, Walt. I would have done anything to stop that."

"And there's no one that you suspect might have the tea set?" His heart softened as he gave the man one last opportunity to be honest.

"No, no one." He lowered his eyes. "But whoever it is, I bet that's probably the person who killed Maryanne." Gerardo glanced back up at Walt. "Too bad we might never know."

"Too bad." Walt nodded, then turned on his heel to walk out. He'd essentially told him that he believed Betty was the killer. But did Gerardo know that? Was it just an attempt to hide his own guilt? Walt couldn't be sure.

CHAPTER 15

Jo spent most of her afternoon watching Betty's villa. Breaking into a residence was a much bigger risk than a business because there was no guarantee that no one would be home at any given time. Instead, she had to wait until she saw Betty leave, and then hope that she wouldn't return too quickly. When she saw Betty step out of her villa, all of her instincts kicked into high gear. If she left on foot, it wouldn't be a good time to break in, but if she left by car then she would hear the car come back and she likely had some time. She wouldn't need much time, though. The villas were fairly small and she just wanted to have a quick look around. Luckily, Betty climbed into her car and drove off.

Jo waited five long minutes to be sure that Betty

wouldn't turn around because she forgot something or changed her mind about going out. Once that time had passed she watched for any signs of neighbors outside or vehicles passing by. Everything was quiet. She walked two villas down and cut through the rear yards to prevent any possibility of someone witnessing her approaching Betty's villa. When she reached Betty's, she peered around the front of the house to see if the car was back. Once she confirmed that no car was there, she crept up to the back door. If she was lucky Betty would be the type of person that didn't lock all of the doors when she left. One jiggle of the doorknob proved that she wasn't. She ran her fingers along the nearby window and gave it an upward shove. It didn't budge. But it did creak. She eyed the lock on the window and saw that it was loose. She gave it another solid shove and the lock gave under the pressure. Betty was cautious, but not cautious enough. As she slipped through the window and into the villa she watched for any signs of pets. There didn't seem to be any as she slid down into the living room.

Everything was in its place, as if perhaps it was never used. She made her way into the bedroom and started in the closet. Most people with something to hide hid it in the closet. She was elbow deep in old suitcases and boxes of clutter when her phone buzzed. Her heart jumped into her throat. How had she made the rookie mistake of not turning her phone off? She grabbed it and was about to turn it off when she saw the message from Eddy.

Betty may have stolen an antique tea set.

Jo stared at the screen for a moment. It was exactly what she needed to know. She could only guess that Eddy and Samantha discovered something about Rose's past. As she switched her phone off, she decided to head into the kitchen before she finished searching in the closet. If she did have a tea set she likely kept it there. When she stepped into the kitchen she noticed that everything was quite a mess. There were drawers and cabinets hanging wide open. The contrast to the neat and tidy living room and bedroom was rather astounding. Without touching much she tried to figure out what Betty might have been up to. Then she heard a sound that made every muscle in her body freeze. Someone was in the pantry just a few feet away from her. Had she been so distracted by the text that she didn't hear Betty come home? Her heart began to pound as she grew dizzy with fear. In all of her years of breaking into places, she'd very rarely nearly been caught.

The sensation of being in a trap threatened to take her breath away. As the person continued to rummage in the pantry she backed slowly out of the kitchen. One glance through the living room window showed that there was still no car in the driveway. Had Betty somehow come home without her car?

"Where is it?" The shout that came from the kitchen made her jump. She ducked down behind the couch and remained there as heavy feet stomped out of the kitchen and towards the bedroom. The voice was definitely masculine, but she wasn't sure who it belonged to. After taking a deep breath she peered around the side of the couch and caught sight of a man just before he stepped into the bedroom. It definitely wasn't Dale. From Walt's description, she guessed that it just might be Gerardo. While he was in the bedroom she took the opportunity to slip back out through the window. Once outside she watched the villa. A few minutes later she saw the man walk right out through the front door. He headed down the sidewalk towards a small car. She was certain that he wasn't supposed to be there, and she noticed that he didn't leave with anything in his hands. She guessed that whatever he came for, he hadn't found.

Just as Jo started back towards her own villa she caught sight of Betty's car coming down the street. She ducked behind a villa before she could be spotted. The man hadn't remained in the house long enough to clean up the mess he made in the kitchen, she was sure of it. She hurried back to her villa, and as she expected, minutes later she heard police sirens wail through the quiet community. As soon as she turned her phone back on she received several texts from her friends both about what they'd found out, and the sirens in the area. Eddy in particular seemed very concerned about her. She texted back that they were welcome to meet at her villa. After she sent the text she began to pace. She'd been in that villa, she'd broken into it. She wore gloves, but she still panicked. What if someone had seen her? She certainly hadn't made the mess, but she was just as guilty as the other intruder. Would the police end up on her doorstep? She felt a little guilty for it, but part of the reason that she asked everyone to come to her villa was to hopefully provide herself with some kind of alibi.

*M*inutes later Jo ushered her friends into her villa.

"Are those sirens about you?" Eddy pulled his hat off and set it down on the back of the couch. "Jo?" He tried to meet her eyes.

"No, they're not. Well, not exactly. That doesn't matter, what does, is that I know who the killer is."

"So do we." Samantha piped up as she settled on a chair.

"It's Gerardo!"

"It's Betty!"

The two women stared at each other with shock.

"Wait a minute. Gerardo?" Walt shook his head. "I don't think he would hurt Maryanne. The way he spoke to me about her was as if he cared about her."

"That may be the case, but while I was breaking into Betty's villa, so was Gerardo. He tore apart her kitchen looking for something."

"The tea set?" Eddy's eyes widened.

"It must have been. Although, something like that would be kept in a safe." Jo shrugged. "I know I didn't find it, and I know he left without anything in his hands. From Walt's description, I'm pretty certain it was Gerardo."

"I know he's a liar, but a killer?" Walt frowned. "My instincts about people must be way off."

"Well, wait a minute. Betty had plenty of motive to kill Maryanne. We suspect that her family may have stolen that tea set from the Marlins."

"I knew it." Walt snapped his fingers. "Gerardo told me that Maryanne was doing tea leaf readings in the area because she wanted to immerse herself in the community because of rumors that someone in the area had her family's stolen tea set. That's why Gerardo called Betty a thief and said he knew what she'd done. He knew that Betty or her father stole the tea set."

"But how did he know?" Samantha narrowed her eyes. "Betty wouldn't have told anyone that she stole it. Somehow Gerardo knew. Do you think she tried to sell it to him?"

"No." Jo shook her head. "No, he knew because Maryanne told him."

"What do you mean?" Eddy looked over at her. "How would she know?"

"Think about it, everyone. I steered us wrong from the beginning. I said that Maryanne's reaction was theatrics, part of a scam. But she wasn't looking at the mound of tea leaves on the saucer, she was looking at the bottom of the cup she had turned over. She must have recognized the cups."

"You're right!" Samantha stood up from her chair. "That makes sense!"

"But why would she tell Gerardo and why wouldn't she have gone to the police?" Eddy frowned. "If she knew that Betty had her cups?"

"The family never reported it stolen." Walt sighed. "That's why. It had been twenty years, and she had no way to prove that Betty had stolen the tea set. Betty also mentioned that they'd gotten to be friends, didn't she? So it's possible that Maryanne wasn't sure if she wanted to get her in trouble. She might have been the forgiving sort."

"It must have been quite a shock to her." Samantha gazed at the floor for a moment. "Someone she probably trusted, might have even considered to be a friend, turned out to be the one who stole from her family."

"And when Betty discovered that Rose was actually Maryanne and that she had figured out that Betty had the stolen tea set, she killed her." Eddy picked up his hat. "It's time to tell Detective Brunner all of this."

"Wait just a minute." Walt stood up as well. "We can't prove any of that. We don't have the tea cups, we don't have proof that Betty or her father stole them, and we have no evidence that Betty caused any harm to Maryanne. The truth is, it could still be Dale, or Gerardo. We're assuming that it was Betty because of the theft, but then why was Gerardo searching Betty's villa? Maybe he wanted the tea set for himself. Maybe he thought that Maryanne had the set and he was going to take it from her. Then discovered she didn't, and went after Betty instead. Or maybe Dale was enraged at the idea that Maryanne wouldn't finish the reading and killed her after all. I mean the murder methods were so similar and the way Dale's wife was killed was never published. How can we be sure of anything?"

"He's right." Eddy set his hat back down. "We may have our suspicions, but without proof we're nowhere."

"How can we get it? I didn't find anything in Betty's house, we can't get near Dale's, and Gerardo is too smart to give anything away." Jo crossed her arms. "We can't just stand by and let one of them get away with it."

"No, we can't." Walt tapped his chin. "I might have an idea."

"Oh?" Eddy turned to face him.

"Maybe we need to have a tea party of our own." He smiled.

"Huh?" Samantha stared at him. "What exactly do you mean?"

"I mean, we should get ourselves invited into Betty's villa again. I'll buy her a special tin of tea, and let Gerardo know that I intend to have it at Betty's. My guess is he'll find an excuse to invite himself as well. We'll all show up on her doorstep, insist on making the tea, then we can hunt down the tea set."

"What if she already sold it?" Samantha frowned.

"No way, I don't think she's already sold it," Jo said. "A tea set like that can't be sold quickly, it's too rare and unique, no one would buy it."

"Then she might have got rid of it." Eddy shrugged.

"Not when it's worth that much money. She is biding her time, trying to find the right buyer, maybe someone foreign, or someone who has a collection of stolen goods. Either way, it will take time." Jo nodded. "I think she still has that tea set, and she probably has it somewhere close. I think this would be our best and last chance at finding out the truth."

"Great, then we'll all meet back at Betty's by four-thirty?" Walt glanced at his watch.

"What if she refuses to let us in?" Eddy adjusted his hat. "We can't just barge in."

"No, we can't, but I'm sure between all of us, we can find a way." Walt's eyes sparkled.

CHAPTER 16

*A*t exactly four-thirty Walt mounted the steps that led to Betty's porch. He had a tin of tea in one hand and a bouquet of flowers in the other. When he knocked on the door, he heard the approach of his friends behind him.

"Walt, are those for me?" Betty smiled as she opened the door.

"Yes, they are. And this tea as well." He displayed the tin of tea. "It's an ancient brew, unique to the Egyptians, and I would like to share it with you."

"You would? Where did you find that?"

"I ordered it specially. I wanted to do something to cheer you up." He smiled as he held out the flowers. "The loss of a friend is not something you can easily overcome, but perhaps with some new friends around to support you, it will not be as difficult." He tipped his head towards Samantha, Eddy, and Jo, as they joined him on the porch.

"You're all here to be my friends?" She laughed a little. "Why?"

"We were there when Rose disappeared, we all saw how upset you were." Samantha shook her head. "You shouldn't have to go through this alone."

"That's why we decided to stage a surprise tea party." Walt patted the tin. "I have the tea, if you have the tea set."

"Oh, I don't know, I just had a break-in and things are still kind of messy." She blushed.

"Sorry to hear that. But it's okay, we don't mind, we can help you tidy up if you would like." Walt stepped forward, and as he'd hoped, Betty naturally stepped back to allow him into the villa. The others soon piled in behind him. Not long after they were seated around the table, a loud knock interrupted their conversation.

"Who could that be?" Betty asked.

"Don't worry, I'll start the tea." Walt walked over to the stove and started the kettle while Betty answered the door.

The others exchanged knowing looks.

"Gerardo, what are you doing here?"

"I'm going to ask you one last time, Betty, where is it? If you don't tell me, I'm going to the police."

"What?" She hissed and stepped outside. The moment she tugged the door shut, Jo sprung into action. She slipped out through the back door and round to the front porch to listen to the conversation.

"Walt came into my shop to buy tea for your little party. He said that you promised to show him an amazing tea set. I know you have it, and I want it!" Gerardo's voice grew darker as he backed Betty against the corner of the porch. "Maryanne said you have it!"

"You're crazy. I never told Walt any of that. He just showed up here with the tea, he said he wanted to cheer me up. I should have known better." She slapped her hand against the porch railing. "The bunch of them are probably trying to pry into my business. Well, I'll teach them some manners."

"Betty, wait." He grabbed her by the arm. "I want the tea set, I mean it. I want to give it back to the Marlins. If you don't give it to me, I'm going to the police and telling them what you did."

"Too late now, Gerardo, the police already asked about what you knew. If you go to them with information now you'll just make yourself look guilty, especially after they find out how many times you called Rose about that stupid tea set. It will look like you were obsessed with her, and you'll be behind bars before you can point your finger at me." She sighed and crossed her arms. "Just relax. Dale is going to jail for Rose's murder. I made sure it would look like he did it. The way he killed his wife was never made public, but I had a friend that worked for the police that mentioned it to me at the time. Given enough time the police will arrest Dale."

"So, you did do it?" He stared at her. "I knew you did, but I just didn't want to believe it."

"Oh, keep quiet, and get off my porch. If I so much as hear a siren, I'm making that call to the police. If I go down, you're going down, too, Gerardo. I'll make sure of it!" She stepped back into the villa and slammed the door shut. Jo hurried back around the house, but before she could get in the back door she heard the lock engage. She ran back around to the front, and found that door was locked as well. Her heart began to race as she realized what was happening. She reached for her phone, only to realize that she'd left it inside on the table. She peered through the front window and saw Betty preparing the tea. She added something to the tea pot just before she carried it to the table.

Jo reached up to pound on the window, but before she could, a hand covered her mouth, and a firm arm wrapped around her body. She flexed and wriggled in his grasp, but he had a tight grip on her.

"Just be quiet." She gasped as he placed his hand over her mouth. Jo became aware that it was Gerardo's voice that whispered in her ear.

~

"That tea smells delicious." Samantha smiled as Betty carried it to the table.

"It does. I'm so lucky that Walt brought this special tea for me. I'm looking forward to trying it." She set a few mugs on the table.

"Oh, I thought you might use the tea set that you used at the tea leaf readings." Walt frowned. "It was such a beautiful set. I wanted a chance to see it again."

"Sorry, no such luck, Walt." She set a mug down in front of him and smiled. "Now, where did Jo go? She was just here, wasn't she?"

"She stepped outside. She should be back any second." Eddy looked towards the front door.

"Oh? All right then, I guess she'll have to join us later. Can't let this tea get cold." She set a mug down in front of Eddy, then one in front of Samantha. "I can't tell you how much it means to me to have such wonderful friends around me. Should we have a toast?" She grabbed a mug for herself.

"First, we must savor this amazing scent." Walt wafted the tea beneath his nose with one hand. "You know, Betty, I've heard rumors that there might be a tea set floating around the area that is worth a lot of money. I'll admit, I suspect it might be the tea set that you had at the reading."

"Do you suspect that?" She smiled as she sat down at the table. "All of you?" She glanced around at each face.

"We're just trying to find out the truth, Betty." Eddy stared her straight in the eye. "A woman is dead, and she deserves justice."

"A woman? Don't you mean a scam artist?" She laughed and waved her hand through the air. "Let's just be honest with each other, who actually believes in tea leaf readings now?"

"Me, maybe." Samantha raised her hand.

"Maybe we should try to do one ourselves." Eddy tapped the side of his mug. "We'll need proper cups to do it."

"Let's all just have our toast." Betty raised her

mug in the air. "To friendship, in whatever form it may come." She took a long sip from her mug.

Walt raised his mug and was about to take a sip, when he noticed something. The scent of the tea was not right. It was the same tea he always drank in the morning, he just packaged it in a special tin. His heart lurched as he realized what must have changed the aroma.

"Don't!" He tossed his tea across the table and grabbed Eddy and Samantha's mugs.

"Walt!" Eddy glared at him as hot tea spilled down the front of his shirt.

"What is it?" Samantha's mug slipped out of her hand and tumbled over on the table.

"You put something in the tea, didn't you?" Walt glared at Betty.

"Just a mild sedative." She shrugged. "It would have made things much easier on all of us." She glanced at her phone, then back up at them. "But then, anyone who fakes a friendship, doesn't really deserve the easy way out, hmm?"

"Is that what Maryanne did to you?" Samantha grabbed some napkins and wiped at Eddy's shirt. "Did it burn you?"

"No, I don't think so." His face was bright red as he pushed the napkins away. "You can't get away with this, Betty. Are you going to kill all of us? Where is Jo?"

"I'm not a killer." She chuckled. "Not anymore, anyway. I'm just going to tuck you and your friends away for a few days, that will give me enough time to disappear. I finally have a buyer for that awful tea set, and soon my father and I will be living in Europe, with all of this behind us."

"You're not putting us anywhere." Eddy lunged up from the table.

"No, no." She held up her phone which displayed a picture of Jo, unconscious. "If anybody puts up a fight, she'll pay the price. It was really stupid of me to use that tea set for the tea leaf readings, but I wanted to help Rose out and she gave me a bigger discount because I did. I offered to set it all up for her and she said she would need a white tea set for the readings. She said that it is easier to see the tea leaves if the cups are white. I decided that it would be special by using that tea set, so I said I had one I could use. I mean what's the point of having something so expensive tucked away. Yes, Rose conned me into thinking she was my friend. But she wasn't. When she saw that tea set at the readings she lost it, she wanted it back. And when she found out the truth she was going to turn me into the police, I know she was. I convinced her to meet me in the empty villa to discuss it, to see if we could reach an agreement. But I knew we wouldn't. I set everything up so that Dale would take the fall. We all know he deserves it, he's a wife killer, who got off on a technicality. No harm done."

"Except Maryanne is dead." Samantha glared at her. "I'd say that's plenty of harm."

"She played with fire." Betty shrugged. "These things happen." She walked over to the back door and unlocked it. Gerardo, with Jo in his arms, stepped inside. "Now, don't overreact." Betty stared hard at Walt, and then Eddy. "She's still alive, for now. I'm going to make us a new batch of tea, and this time you're going to drink it. The sedative will be much kinder to you than being knocked out by force, don't you think?" She smiled as she filled the kettle with water again.

"Detective Brunner will figure this out, Betty. You're better off trying to make a deal." Eddy took a small step towards her.

"Detective Brunner will think whatever I tell him to think. I will hand him Dale on a silver platter and he will be all too happy to close the case. After all, he'll be too busy looking for you and your friends, won't he?" She laughed.

"What should I do with her?" Gerardo adjusted Jo in his arms. "She's getting heavy."

"Just toss her anywhere. I'll get some sedative in her for good measure." Betty shrugged.

The kettle began to shriek. The sudden sharp sound made everyone jump. Walt gazed at Jo as Gerardo started to carry her over to the couch. He suddenly shoved Samantha back behind the table, and lunged towards Betty.

"Walt, what are you doing?" Eddy reached for his arm to stop him, but before he could grasp it, Walt had his hand over Betty's on the boiling kettle. In the living room, Gerardo was met with a hard stomp of Jo's heel to his foot. He screamed almost as loud as the kettle.

"What did you do that for?" Gerardo exclaimed.

"Insurance," Jo said.

As Gerardo held onto his foot hopping on one leg, Betty struggled to escape Walt.

"I'll pour this on you!" She tugged at the tea kettle. "It'll burn!"

"I'm not afraid of you." Walt growled and tugged the tea kettle harder. Betty struggled to escape Walt.

"Enough!" Eddy exclaimed. Samantha rushed forward and grabbed one of the mugs from the table as she did. She slammed it hard against the top of Betty's head and Eddy grabbed the tea kettle out of both of their hands and tossed it into the sink. "You will stay right here until Detective Brunner gets here." Eddy wrapped his arm around Betty's waist.

"I'll do no such thing!" She shrieked and flung herself back and forth in an attempt to get out of his grasp.

Samantha was already on the phone calling the police, when Jo stepped forward, and glared at Betty.

"This is what real friendship is, in case you were wondering. It's not something you can buy, or con."

"You have nothing on me! Nothing!" She screeched.

"No?" Gerardo took his phone out of his pocket. "Too bad I never turned off the video chat. Everything from the moment I connected with you has been recorded, I'm sure the police will find it quite interesting."

"Gerardo, what did you do?" Betty asked.

"The right thing. I pretended to knock Jo out so you would let us in here," Gerardo said as he handed his phone to Eddy.

"You are going to pay for what you did, Gerardo!" Betty exclaimed. "You traitor!"

"I never could have believed that you would murder Maryanne, but now I know it's true." Gerardo frowned. "When she came to me after the reading party and told me about the cups, I should have done something then. I couldn't let you kill anyone else. This footage will not only put you behind bars, but will ultimately clear my name of the murder as well."

"Just toss the phone, we can work this out." Betty pleaded as she looked back at Eddy. "Do you really want Dale to continue to be free?"

"Whether or not Dale is innocent I don't know, I know for certain that you are guilty." Eddy continued to hold her tight. "And you are going to pay for what you've done."

CHAPTER 17

The sound of sirens filled the air as Betty was led out of the villa for questioning. Gerardo was in the corner being interviewed by an officer. Jo waved away the EMT that attempted to check her vital signs.

"I'm fine. I wasn't even knocked out." Jo snapped her teeth. "And I bite."

"He's only trying to help." Samantha tossed her arm around Jo's shoulders.

"How did you know, Walt?" Jo asked.

"When the tea kettle whistled, I saw your eyes flutter, and I knew you were waiting for the right moment to attack." Walt smiled as he studied her. "I didn't know it was all an act though. I really thought Gerardo had knocked you out."

"It's embarrassing that Gerardo got the upper

hand on me in the first place, and was able to come up behind and restrain me before he told me his plans. I just didn't expect it. I must be getting rusty." She sighed.

"Thanks to Walt's educated sniffer, we weren't all knocked out." Eddy shuddered. "I hate to think what might have happened if it weren't for that. How did you know, Walt?"

"I drink this tea almost every morning. The only time I miss it is when I'm on vacation. I sniff it, every morning. I never really thought I memorized the smell so closely. I never paid attention to trying to remember it. But when that tea hit my nose I realized that there was something off. Jo hadn't come back, and Betty was being far too friendly. My best guess was that she had added something to the tea. But that was all it was, a guess." He pushed his glasses up along his nose. "We're lucky it all turned out so well for us."

"Yes, for us, but not for Maryanne." Samantha frowned. "She's gone, and she didn't even get to fulfill one of her father's last wishes. Who knows where the tea set is?"

"I might be able to help with that." Walt walked over to the cabinet beside the oven. "I store my kettle and my tea in this cabinet at home. It's the easiest to reach. I noticed that Betty had to get her kettle from a cabinet on the other side of the kitchen, and she didn't put the tin of tea away. Let's see why she didn't use this cabinet." He pulled open the door. Each of the shelves inside was empty. "Oh well, I guess I'm not always right." He smiled.

"Maybe in this one?" Samantha popped the next cabinet open. It was filled with plates and glasses. "I guess not."

"No, but..." Walt stared into the cabinet. "It's far deeper than the first one." He pulled the other cabinet door open again. "Yes, this cabinet should be deeper. The kitchens are fairly uniform in all of the villas." He knocked on the interior wall of the cabinet. A hollow sound echoed back. With a grin he pushed on the back of the cabinet. The thin wood came loose, and he pulled it away. Behind it was a tea set, the tea set that had been used on the day of the tea leaf readings.

"Here it is, Maryanne," he whispered.

"I'm sure her father will be so pleased to have it back." Jo slipped her hand into Walt's. "You've done a good thing here, Walt."

"We all have." Walt glanced around at them. "Maryanne's murder is solved, and we can all be proud of our part in that. It didn't take a tea leaf reading, just our own instincts."

"I'm not sure I'll ever be able to look at tea the same way again." Eddy scrunched up his nose. "After almost being poisoned."

"Ah, but that wasn't the tea's fault. Don't worry, Eddy, I'll help you through this." Walt clapped Eddy on the back.

Eddy was startled for a second. Walt had never clapped him on the back before.

Eddy took his phone out to text Detective Brunner to ensure he knew what was happening. As he looked at the screen he realized he had missed a text from the detective.

We just solved the murder of Dale's wife. We decided to reopen the case and use DNA tests that weren't available at the time. It turns out that Dale is innocent. It was his wife's ex-fiancé that killed her. Apparently, he was upset when she called off the wedding and harbored the grudge for years.

Eddy smiled as he read the text to his friends.

As the four friends stepped outside to meet up with Detective Brunner, Sage Gardens was once again glowing with flashing lights. But at least this time, a sense of safety and well-being had been restored.

"So much for intuition." Samantha smiled as she

leaned in close to Eddy and tried to hide from the crowd of onlookers.

"You knew it was Betty, didn't you?" He eyed her for a moment. "Whether it's intuition, instincts, or good old fashioned dumb luck, I'll always trust your hunches, Samantha."

"Thanks Eddy." She rested her head on his shoulder. "But I'd rather you didn't. A good amount of doubt just makes me work harder to prove that I'm right."

"Ah, I see." He grinned. "I'll keep that in mind."

"Eddy?" Detective Brunner walked up to him, and looked over the others gathered close. "Is anyone going to explain all of this to me?"

"Sure we will, Detective." Walt cleared his throat. "Would you like to join us for a cup of tea?"

The End

ALSO BY CINDY BELL

DUNE HOUSE COZY MYSTERIES

BEKKI THE BEAUTICIAN COZY MYSTERIES

Mistletoe, Makeup and Murder

Hairpin, Hair Dryer and Homicide

Blush, a Bride and a Body

Shampoo and a Stiff

Cosmetics, a Cruise and a Killer

Lipstick, a Long Iron and Lifeless

Camping, Concealer and Criminals

Treated and Dyed

A Wrinkle-Free Murder

SAGE GARDENS COZY MYSTERIES

Birthdays Can Be Deadly

Money Can Be Deadly

Trust Can Be Deadly

Ties Can Be Deadly

Rocks Can Be Deadly

Jewelry Can Be Deadly

Numbers Can Be Deadly

Memories Can Be Deadly

Paintings Can Be Deadly

Snow Can Be Deadly

CHOCOLATE CENTERED COZY MYSTERIES

The Sweet Smell of Murder

A Deadly Delicious Delivery

A Bitter Sweet Murder

A Treacherous Tasty Trail

Luscious Pastry at a Lethal Party

Trouble and Treats

Fudge Films and Felonies

Custom-Made Murder

WENDY THE WEDDING PLANNER COZY MYSTERIES

Matrimony, Money and Murder

Chefs, Ceremonies and Crimes

Knives and Nuptials

Mice, Marriage and Murder

ABOUT THE AUTHOR

Cindy Bell is the author of the cozy mystery series Donut Truck, Dune House, Sage Gardens, Chocolate Centered, Macaron Patisserie, Nuts about Nuts, Bekki the Beautician, Heavenly Highland Inn and Wendy the Wedding Planner.

Cindy has always loved reading, but it is only recently that she has discovered her passion for writing romantic cozy mysteries. She loves walking along the beach thinking of the next adventure her characters can embark on.

You can sign up for her newsletter so you are notified of her latest releases at http://www.cindybellbooks.com.

Made in the USA
Las Vegas, NV
21 November 2024

12277140R00125